DEATH ON THE BOOKSHELF

PAGES AND PAWS
BOOK 1

POPPY BRIDGEMAN

Ebook ISBN: 978-1-990509-67-4
Paperback ISBN: 978-1-990509-68-1
Audio book ISBN:978-1-990509-69-8

Cover by Get Covers

FREE BOOK

Claim your copy of The Charleston Diary when you sign up for my newsletter. Learn how Ginny solved a case of forgery before she headed to the peace and tranquility of Tidehaven Cove.

1

I stared up at the weathered sign swinging gently in the morning breeze. Hampton's Books. The gold lettering had faded to a pale yellow, and the wood had darkened with age, but there was still something magical about seeing my own surname on a bookshop in a quaint Devon village. My bookshop. The thought still didn't feel real.

"Come on, you two," I murmured, tugging gently at the tangled leashes wrapped around my ankles. Austen and Hardy looked up at me with identical expressions of corgi impatience. Six days in England, and they were already acting like they owned the place. Hardy gave a small, insistent woof.

"I know, I know. Just let me..." I fumbled with the ring of ancient keys the solicitor had given me yesterday, trying to match the tarnished brass to the equally tarnished lock. The largest key slid in but refused to turn. Jet lag clouded my thoughts, making the simple task monumentally difficult. It was—I checked my watch—8:48 AM. Far too early after a night of ceiling-staring insomnia, but I'd been too excited to stay at the cottage a minute longer.

I jiggled the key, pushing harder. Nothing.

"You have to lift the door slightly while you turn it," came a crisp voice from behind me.

I startled, nearly dropping the keys. A tall, thin man in his late sixties stood watching my struggles with a mixture of disapproval and resignation. He wore a tweed jacket despite the mild spring morning and carried a leather satchel that had seen better decades.

"Oh! Thank you. Are you..." I awkwardly hoisted the door up with my knee while turning the key, and the lock finally clicked open.

"Malcolm Blackwood. Assistant manager." He reached past me to push the door inward, revealing the shop's dimly lit interior. "Though I've been running things since your great-aunt took ill. You're late."

I blinked in confusion as the dogs darted inside, their nails clicking against the wooden floor. "Late? But the shop doesn't open until nine. I checked the hours posted in the window."

Malcolm pulled out a pocket watch and consulted it with theatrical precision. "Mrs. Hampton-Davies always arrived at precisely eight-thirty. For thirty years." He managed to make this sound like both a sacred tradition and a personal failing on my part. "I've already opened up. Just stepped outside for a small personal task. I have my own key."

Of course he did. I suppressed a sigh and followed him inside, inhaling the distinctive scent of old books, furniture polish, and something indefinably British. Dust motes danced in the shafts of light coming through the bay windows. Even in my jet-lagged state, the sight made my heart lift. Crowded shelves stretched toward the ceiling, creating a maze of literary treasures that was simultaneously overwhelming and thrilling.

"I'll put the kettle on," Malcolm continued, moving behind an imposing wooden counter that dominated the front of the shop. "Mrs. Hampton-Davies always took her tea with one sugar and a splash of milk. I assume you'll want the same."

"Actually, I usually drink coffee in the mornings. Black." I set my bag down next to the ancient brass cash register that gleamed with recent polishing. "And please, call me Ginny. Mrs. Hampton-Davies was my great-aunt Vivian."

Malcolm pursed his lips as if I'd suggested something faintly improper. "Perhaps Miss Hampton would be more appropriate. The customers expect a certain... decorum."

Before I could respond, a crash from the back of the shop made us both turn. Hardy emerged from between two bookshelves looking pleased with himself, while a neat stack of leather-bound volumes now lay scattered across the floor.

"The dogs," Malcolm said faintly, as if he'd just noticed two corgi-shaped catastrophes invading his domain. "They'll be staying at your cottage during working hours, of course?"

I hurried over to restack the books. "Actually, I thought they could stay here at the shop. Great for customer engagement, you know? People love dogs in bookstores. There's research showing they increase browsing time by nearly twenty percent."

The look on Malcolm's face suggested I'd proposed filling the rare book room with mud.

"Mrs. Hampton-Davies was allergic to all animals," he said stiffly. "We've never had pets in the shop."

I straightened up, books neatly arranged again. "Well, I'm not allergic, and from my great-aunt's letters, I got the impression this place could use a little boost in foot traffic. The dogs stay." I softened my tone. "They're very well-behaved, normally. It's just the new environment."

As if to contradict me, Austen jumped onto a worn leather armchair, turned three precise circles, and settled herself as if she'd been sleeping there all her life.

Malcolm's mouth opened and closed without sound, then he turned and disappeared into a small alcove. I heard the decisive click of a kettle being set down with more force than necessary.

Day one, minute five: already offended the long-time employee, I thought, surveying the shop. Great start.

My gaze fell on the brass cash register again. It was beautiful, a museum piece really, but completely impractical for a modern business. I'd need to install a proper point-of-sale system immediately. Just another item for the growing mental list of updates the place desperately needed.

In my previous life—was it only two weeks ago?—I'd been senior editor at a respected publishing house in Charlotte, making snap decisions about commercial viability and market trends. Busy, efficient, deadline-driven. The opposite of this sleepy shop in a village where time seemed to move more slowly.

Before I could contemplate this further, Malcolm reappeared with a steaming cup of tea, which he placed on the counter with the precision of someone handling nitro-glycerin.

"Your great-aunt's morning tea," he announced, making it clear I had no choice in the matter. "The tea things live here, they've always lived here." He gestured to the specific spot on the counter, as if the teacup might spontaneously migrate if not warned against such behavior.

"Thank you," I said, deciding to choose my battles. I took a sip and was surprised by the perfect balance of sweet and bitter. "This is actually really good."

Malcolm acknowledged this with the slightest nod, then opened the leather satchel to extract a small notebook. "Now, regarding today's business. We have a regular order to prepare for Mrs. Abernathy. Dickens, she's working through the complete set. The historical society requested we set aside any new arrivals pertaining to local maritime history."

My fingers itched to pull out my laptop and create a proper spreadsheet. "Do we have an inventory system? A database of customers and their preferences?"

Malcolm tapped the notebook meaningfully. "Everything is here, Miss Hampton. As it has been for thirty years."

"Digital backup would be—"

"Unnecessary," he finished, with the finality of someone closing a particularly dull book. "Now, if you'll excuse me, I need to prepare the section displays before opening."

As he moved away, the shop's old telephone rang. I reached for it, but Malcolm materialized beside me with startling speed.

"Hampton's Books, good morning," he intoned, then his expression darkened. "Yes, she's here. One moment." He held out the receiver to me with the enthusiasm of someone passing along a dead mouse. "Oliver Blackthorn. The antiques dealer."

I took the phone. "Hello, this is Ginny Hampton."

"Ah, the American heiress!" The voice on the other end was jovial with an undertone of calculation. "Welcome to our little village. I just wanted to introduce myself as your business neighbor. Perhaps we could meet for lunch? There's my standing offer to discuss, of course."

"Standing offer?"

"For the building," Oliver continued smoothly. "Your great-aunt and I had numerous conversations about my interest in expanding my antiques business. Prime corner location, you see. I've always felt books and antiques would make a rather seamless transition."

I watched Malcolm arranging books with sharp, agitated movements, clearly eavesdropping.

"I'm not looking to sell, Mr. Blackthorn. I've just arrived."

"Oliver, please! And of course, of course. Just getting my name in early. The old place must seem quite overwhelming for someone used to... American efficiency." He made it sound like a mild disease. "The maintenance alone on these listed buildings can be ruinous."

Listed building? I felt a headache forming behind my eyes. Of course it would be historically protected. That would complicate my modernization plans.

"I'll keep that in mind, but I'm really not—"

"We'll talk soon," Oliver interrupted cheerfully. "Can't wait to meet those American ideas of yours. Cheerio!"

The line went dead, and I replaced the receiver with more force than necessary.

"Vultures circling already," Malcolm muttered, suddenly beside me again. "That man has been trying to get his hands on this shop for years. Developers and their schemes, no respect for literary heritage."

I was about to reply when I noticed a small slip of paper sticking out of the cash register drawer. I pulled it free. A handwritten note in elegant script read: "Tuesday - R.T. - back room - NO." The last word was underlined three times.

"What's this?" I asked, holding up the note.

Malcolm snatched it with surprising speed. "Nothing of importance. Old business."

"Who's R.T.?"

"No one you need concern yourself with." He tucked the note into his pocket, his expression closing like a book. "Now, perhaps you'd like to familiarize yourself with the rare book room? The key is kept in the second drawer, though of course I'll need to accompany you."

The bell above the door jingled, and both of us turned to see a plump woman with silver-streaked hair bustling in, carrying a tray covered with a checkered cloth.

"Good morning, good morning!" she trilled. "I saw the lights on and thought our new American friend might appreciate a proper welcome!" She set the tray on the counter, revealing a teapot, cups, and a plate of scones still steaming from the oven. "Elspeth Willoughby, dear. I run the tea shop across the way."

Her bright eyes examined me with unconcealed curiosity. "You must be the great-niece! Vivian mentioned you, of course, though she never said you'd inherit the shop. Such a surprise to everyone! Do tell us what brings you all the way from America. Charlotte, isn't it? North Carolina? I've never been, but my second cousin traveled to Atlanta once and found it quite alarming."

I opened my mouth, but Elspeth continued without pause.

"And these must be your little dogs! How perfectly charming. We've never had dogs in the shop before, have we, Malcolm? Such a refreshing change. Vivian was terribly allergic, you know, broke out in the most alarming hives. But you must tell me everything about yourself. Have you left family behind? A special someone, perhaps? What made you decide to take on a bookshop, of all things?"

The rapid-fire personal questions made me instinctively retreat behind my professional smile—the one I'd perfected during tedious publishing cocktail parties.

"It's lovely to meet you, Ms. Willoughby. Thank you for the welcome treats."

"Elspeth, dear. We're all so informal here." She leaned closer, voice dropping to a stage whisper. "Except Malcolm, of course. Haven't seen him use a first name since 1997."

Malcolm cleared his throat pointedly and moved away to straighten books that were already perfectly aligned.

"I'm still settling in," I continued, deliberately vague. "The time difference is quite an adjustment."

"Of course, of course. But you must come for a proper tea soon, tell us all about your American publishing career. Word gets around, you know! And I make the best Victoria sponge in Devon—won the village fête three years running until that business with the judges' voting system."

Elspeth's gaze traveled around the shop with the precision of someone cataloging every detail for later discussion. "I see you haven't made any changes yet. Bold of you to have the dogs in, though. People will talk!"

They already are, I'm sure, I thought. Out loud I said, "I'm taking my time to understand how everything works before making decisions."

"Sensible! Though between us"—Elspeth lowered her voice again—"a little updating wouldn't go amiss. Had my eye on that old armchair for ages, simply crawling with dust mites, I'd wager." She straightened up. "Well, I'll leave you to it! Shop to open, gossip—I mean news—to share. Do pop over any time!"

With a cheery wave, she was gone in a cloud of floral perfume, leaving behind the scent of fresh scones and thinly veiled inquisition.

I sank into the supposedly mite-infested armchair, only to find Austen already occupying half of it. Hardy promptly flopped across my feet like a furry doorstop.

"Harbingers of change," Malcolm said darkly, eyeing the dogs. "Mrs. Hampton-Davies would never have allowed it."

I stroked Austen's soft head. "Change isn't always bad, Malcolm."

"Hmph." He adjusted his bow tie with dignity. "I'll be in the history section if you need me, Miss Hampton."

Left alone at last, I surveyed my domain with a mixture of delight and trepidation. Across the Atlantic, I'd imagined this moment differently—a triumphant fresh start, away from office politics and the lingering embarrassment of a broken engagement. Reality, as usual, was messier. I'd inherited not just a bookshop but decades of traditions, an employee who clearly resented me, and neighbors who saw me as the latest village entertainment.

I took another sip of the now-lukewarm tea. One step at a time. Rome wasn't built in a day, and Hampton's Books wouldn't be revolutionized in one either.

The peaceful moment was shattered by the telephone ringing again. I stood and reached for it, but the sound stopped abruptly. Malcolm must have answered the extension upstairs. A few moments later, I heard his footsteps on the wooden stairs.

"A customer inquiry about opening hours," he said, though something in his tight expression suggested otherwise. "Nothing important."

I nodded, choosing not to press. I'd learn the rhythms of this place eventually. Pulling my laptop from my bag, I opened it on the counter, pointedly ignoring Malcolm's disapproving glance.

"I'm going to start a proper inventory," I announced. "And maybe look into getting some social media set up for the shop."

"We have a telephone and a mailbox," Malcolm replied.

"Mrs. Hampton-Davies found them perfectly adequate for sixty years."

Before I could formulate a diplomatic response, a loud thud from the second floor made us both look up.

"What was that?" I asked.

Malcolm's expression flickered momentarily before settling back into professional neutrality. "Old buildings make noises, Miss Hampton. One gets used to it."

"It sounded like books falling."

"Perhaps." His tone discouraged further questioning. "If you'll excuse me, I need to check the new arrivals that came in yesterday."

As he disappeared into the back room, I felt the first tendrils of unease creeping up my spine. The noise had sounded very much like deliberate movement, not random settling. And Malcolm's reaction...

Hardy suddenly raised his head, ears pricked toward the ceiling. He gave a low, uncertain whine.

"Just old building noises," I reassured him, echoing Malcolm's words with more confidence than I felt. "Nothing to worry about."

But as I turned back to my laptop, I couldn't shake the feeling that someone—or something—was moving around in the supposedly empty rooms above. Welcome to England, indeed.

2

I arrived at the bookshop at precisely 8:45 the next morning, a time I'd calculated with strategic precision —late enough to assert my authority, early enough to appear responsible. Malcolm was already inside, his gaze fixed on his pocket watch like a disappointed schoolmaster.

"Good morning, Malcolm," I said brightly, ignoring his theatrical sigh as he returned the watch to his waistcoat pocket.

"Miss Hampton," he murmured with a small nod. "We generally open at nine, which means preparations should be complete by then."

I hung my coat on the rack by the door. "And they will be. I just need to get Austen and Hardy settled."

The corgis trotted in behind me, Austen immediately inspecting the perimeter of the sales floor while Hardy made a beeline for the hearth rug. Malcolm watched them with thinly veiled disapproval.

"Mrs. Hampton-Davies never kept animals in the shop."

"I'm not my great-aunt," I replied, a phrase I suspected I'd be repeating often. "And they're very well-behaved. Mostly."

As if on cue, Hardy flopped onto his back, legs splayed in a decidedly undignified position. Malcolm sniffed.

The shop door burst open with enough force to set the brass bell clanging wildly. A whirlwind of purple cardigan and flying papers swept in.

"So sorry I'm late! The bus was absolutely packed with schoolchildren and then Mrs. Willberry asked me about my thesis and you know how she goes on and—oh!"

The girl skidded to a halt, nearly colliding with a display of local history books. She appeared to be in her early twenties, with a riot of dark curls pulled into a messy bun and wide brown eyes magnified by oversized glasses. Several pencils protruded from her hair at odd angles.

"You must be Miss Hampton! I'm Freya Collins! Part-time assistant and full-time literature student! It's absolutely brilliant to meet you!" She thrust out a hand adorned with mismatched rings.

I accepted the enthusiastic handshake. "Please, call me Ginny. And you're not late. I only just arrived myself."

"Eight forty-seven," Malcolm muttered without looking up from the morning's receipts.

Freya's eyes widened further. "Oh no, I'm usually here by eight-thirty to help Malcolm with the morning routine. Did you manage the kettle all right? He's very particular about—"

"I've survived thus far without tea," Malcolm interrupted. "Though one wonders how long that can continue."

"I'll get it started right away," Freya said, hurrying toward the small alcove that housed the tea-making supplies. "Do you take milk, Miss—Ginny? Sugar? I can never remember how Americans take their tea. Or do you prefer coffee? I could run across to Elspeth's if—"

"Tea is fine," I said, feeling slightly breathless just listening to her. "Milk, no sugar."

"Perfect! Malcolm takes his with just a splash of milk, precisely one teaspoon of sugar, and the bag left in for exactly two and a half minutes. Any longer and it's too strong, any shorter and it's dishwater, isn't that right, Malcolm?"

The older man's expression softened almost imperceptibly. "Indeed."

As Freya bustled about with teacups and saucers, I watched the strange dance of the two staff members. Despite their obvious differences, there was a comfortable rhythm to their interactions that made me feel distinctly out of step.

"So," I said, "perhaps you two could fill me in on the usual daily routine?"

Malcolm and Freya exchanged a look that made me feel like I'd suggested rewriting classic literature in emoji.

"Well," Freya began, "we open at nine, of course, but Malcolm's usually here by seven-thirty to—"

"Seven precisely," he corrected.

"Seven, right, to check the registers and sort any special orders. I arrive at eight-thirty to prepare the tea and dust the displays. The post comes at ten-fifteen, except on Wednesdays when it's eleven because Roger has his chiropodist appointment, which means we need to sort new deliveries by—"

"Eleven-thirty," Malcolm finished. "Allowing precisely one hour before lunch."

"Which is always twelve-thirty to one-thirty," Freya continued, "though Malcolm usually stays in to mind the shop while I go out, then I take over at—"

"One-thirty precisely," Malcolm said, "allowing me thirty minutes for a constitutional around the village green."

"Then we have the afternoon lull between two and three, which is when we do the inventory count for the day and arrange any new displays."

"The school children arrive at three forty-five," Malcolm added with a slight grimace.

"They're really very sweet," Freya insisted. "And potential future customers!"

"Future vandals, more likely," Malcolm muttered.

"And then we close at five-thirty, except on Thursdays when we stay open until seven for the book club, and Saturdays when we close at four because the village basically shuts down early for the pub quiz."

I blinked, trying to absorb the intricate timetable. In Charlotte, my publishing schedule had been managed with digital calendars, automated reminders, and a personal assistant. Here, it seemed to exist entirely in Malcolm and Freya's heads, a complex choreography of village rhythms I couldn't yet hear.

"I see," I said, though I didn't really. "And what about online orders or—"

The bell above the door jangled with enough force to cut me off mid-sentence. A tall, angular man strode in, his tweed jacket and silver-topped walking stick giving him the air of a country squire despite the sleek modern watch glinting at his wrist. His frown deepened when he spotted me.

"Ah. The American arrival. Oliver Blackthorn." He extended a manicured hand that matched his clipped introduction. "Blackthorn's Antiques, two doors down."

"Ginny Hampton. Nice to meet you in person."

His handshake was brief and cool. "We spoke yesterday. Regarding my standing offer."

"I'm afraid I'm not—"

"For the property," he spoke over me, his gaze sweeping the shop with the calculating assessment of an estate agent. "I've been trying to expand for years. This corner location would be ideal. Your aunt always refused, of course, but I thought with new ownership..."

Malcolm appeared at my elbow with surprising stealth. "Mr. Blackthorn, we're not actually open for another seven minutes."

Oliver ignored him completely. "I'm prepared to make a very generous offer. The book business is dying, after all. E-readers, online retailers." He gestured vaguely toward the shelves. "All this is rather... quaint, but hardly profitable."

I felt a surge of protectiveness toward the shop that surprised me with its intensity. "I'm not interested in selling."

"You haven't heard my offer."

"I don't need to. The shop isn't for sale."

Oliver's smile didn't reach his eyes. "You Americans are always so... decisive. Perhaps give it a few months. The charm of village life can wear thin, especially when the books aren't selling and the roof starts leaking."

"Is there something specific you needed today, Mr. Blackthorn?" I asked, maintaining my polite smile with effort. "A book, perhaps?"

He chuckled as if I'd made a joke. "Books are only valuable when they're old enough to be antiques, my dear. Speaking of which, if you do find anything of real value tucked away in those dusty corners, do let me know. I'm always in the market for genuine antiquities."

"We'll be sure to keep that in mind," I said.

After he left, I turned to Malcolm. "Is he always that—"

"Insufferable? Indeed." Malcolm straightened a row of books with precise movements. "He's been trying to get his hands on this property for years. Developers and their schemes."

"I'm not selling the shop," I said firmly.

Malcolm gave me a long look. "We shall see."

The morning passed in a blur of customers, questions, and countless cups of tea. I was surprised by the steady stream of villagers who seemed to visit less for books than to inspect the new American owner. Each brought their own version of the same questions: How was I finding Tidehaven Cove? Wasn't it different from America? Did I know my great-aunt well? How long did I plan to stay?

I deflected the personal questions with vague responses and redirected conversations to books whenever possible. By lunchtime, my cheeks ached from maintaining my polite smile.

As Freya departed for lunch, practically bouncing out the door with energy that seemed inexhaustible, I took the opportunity to examine the sales ledger. Flipping through Malcolm's meticulous handwriting, I noticed the same notation appearing several times: "R.T. - back room."

"Malcolm," I called, "what does this mean? The 'R.T.' entries?"

He appeared so quickly I wondered if he'd been hovering nearby. "Private appointments," he said stiffly. "Nothing that concerns—"

The shop bell jangled again, and Malcolm's expression darkened so rapidly that I turned in surprise.

3

A man stood in the doorway, thin and stooped with watery blue eyes magnified by wire-rimmed spectacles. His tweed jacket with leather elbow patches and the worn leather satchel clutched to his chest screamed "academic" so loudly that I half-expected him to be carrying a pipe.

"Miss Hampton, I presume?" The man's smile didn't reach his eyes as he stepped forward. "Dr. Reginald Thornbury. Local historian and antiquarian book specialist. I had an appointment with your great-aunt before her... unfortunate passing."

R.T., I thought, glancing back at the ledger.

"That appointment is canceled," Malcolm said sharply.

Thornbury ignored him, focusing entirely on me. "I've been conducting essential research on Devon's maritime history. Your great-aunt kindly agreed to allow me access to certain manuscripts in your archives."

"We have no such arrangement," Malcolm insisted, his usually proper demeanor slipping. "And I'll thank you to leave immediately."

I placed a calming hand on Malcolm's arm. "Dr. Thornbury, I'm happy to discuss any research materials, but—as you can see, I'm still getting settled. Perhaps next week—"

"This can't wait," Thornbury snapped. He reached into his satchel and withdrew a sheaf of documents. "I have here the written correspondence between myself and Mrs. Hampton-Davies, clearly indicating her agreement to grant me access to the 1843 Harbormaster's Journal, which I have reason to believe is stored in your rare book room."

He thrust the papers toward me, which I took reflexively.

"Those are forgeries," Malcolm hissed.

"They most certainly are not," Thornbury replied, his scholarly facade cracking. "Mrs. Hampton-Davies understood the academic importance of my work, even if her watchdog did not."

I skimmed the documents, noting the formal language and what appeared to be my great-aunt's signature. The letters were dated just a month before her death.

"I don't doubt your work is important, Dr. Thornbury," I said carefully, "but I need time to verify these arrangements. As you can imagine, I'm still sorting through my great-aunt's affairs."

"The material I seek is time-sensitive. There's a publishing deadline—"

"That sounds like a personal problem," Malcolm muttered.

Thornbury's face flushed. "I've been more than patient! That journal belongs in proper academic hands, not gathering dust in some provincial bookshop run by an American who probably can't distinguish between a first edition and a paperback reprint!"

One of my corporate skills had been de-escalating tense situations, usually between authors with inflated egos and editors with deflated budgets. I stepped forward, positioning myself subtly between Malcolm and Thornbury.

"Dr. Thornbury, I understand your frustration, but I've only just arrived. I need to familiarize myself with the shop's archives before granting anyone access, no matter what previous arrangements might have been discussed. I'd be happy to review your request next week and—"

"This is completely unacceptable!" Thornbury snatched the papers from my hands. "You'll regret not cooperating, Miss... Hampton. Mark my words."

He stormed out, the bell clanging violently in his wake. Through the window, I could see him gesticulating furiously as he walked away.

"Well," I said, turning to Malcolm, "that was—"

"That man," Malcolm said with surprising venom, "is not welcome here. He's been trying to get his hands on our rare books collection for years."

"Does he have a legitimate research interest?"

Malcolm's expression suggested I'd asked if Jack the Ripper had a legitimate interest in surgery. "He claims to be writing a definitive history of Devon's maritime trade, but what he really wants is the Harbormaster's Journal because it contains navigational charts that supposedly identify the location of the Maria Constance wreck."

"The what?"

"A merchant vessel that sank in 1843, allegedly carrying a substantial cargo of gold and antiquities. The ship's exact location has never been found, but treasure hunters have been searching for generations."

I raised an eyebrow. "And you think Dr. Thornbury is a treasure hunter rather than a historian?"

"What I think," Malcolm said precisely, "is that Reginald

Thornbury would sell his own mother for the right price, and we should not allow him anywhere near the archives."

The vehemence in his tone surprised me. Malcolm had been cool and proper since my arrival, but this was the first real emotion I'd seen from him. Well, apart from polite disdain of me and my modern ways.

"Was my great-aunt aware of this theory about the journal?"

"Mrs. Hampton-Davies was an excellent judge of character," Malcolm replied, which wasn't exactly an answer.

Before I could press further, the bell jangled again. This time it announced a small, round woman with silver curls and apple-red cheeks, carrying a basket covered with a checkered cloth.

"Yoo-hoo! Just popping by with a little welcome gift!" she called in a voice that suggested 'inside' and 'outside' volumes were identical. "I'm Dorothy Jenkins—call me Dot—your neighbor to the left!" She thrust the basket toward me. "Homemade preserves! The strawberry's a bit runny this year but the blackberry won a commendation at the village fête last summer!"

"That's very kind, thank you," I said, accepting the surprisingly heavy basket.

"No trouble at all! Neighbors should look after each other," Dot replied, making no move to leave. Her bright eyes scanned the shop before landing back on me. "I saw that Thornbury man leaving in quite a state. Causing trouble already, is he?"

Malcolm muttered something about inventory and retreated to the back of the shop.

"Oh no, just a small misunderstanding," I said, unwilling to fuel village gossip on my second day.

"Oh, I'm sure." Dot nodded knowingly. "He was always

pestering your great-aunt about those old books of hers. Claimed he needed them for his research, but we all know he's after that sunken treasure."

So much for not fueling village gossip.

"Was that Thornbury I saw stomping away like a petulant child?" The new voice came from the doorway, where a tall, austere man with silver-touched temples stood regarding us with mild air of superiority. "I do hope he's not bothering you about that ridiculous shipwreck theory again."

"Dr. Penrose," Dot greeted him with exaggerated formality. "Decided to grace the village with your presence today, have you?"

The man ignored her entirely, addressing me instead. "Nathaniel Penrose. I'm your neighbor to the right. Those dogs of yours were barking excessively this morning."

I glanced at Austen and Hardy, who were both sound asleep on the hearth rug. "I'm sorry to hear that. They're usually very quiet."

"Well, they weren't at six a.m. Some of us are trying to work."

"I apologize. I'll make sure they're not left alone in the garden early in the morning."

Dr. Penrose gave a curt nod. "See that you do. And don't let Thornbury bully you. He's no more a proper historian than I am a circus performer."

"He's not a proper anything," Dot stage-whispered. "Did you know he tried to pass off Elspeth's grandmother's pudding recipe as a 'medieval discovery' in that book of his? Poor Elspeth nearly had apoplexy when she saw it in print."

"Elspeth mentioned she had some history with Thornbury," I recalled, thinking of her visit yesterday.

"Oh, she would have told you all about it, I'm sure. That

woman doesn't let a grudge die quietly." Dot glanced toward the door. "Speaking of which, I'm surprised she hasn't popped in again already. She usually makes her rounds by—"

The bell jangled again. The plump, silver-haired figure of Elspeth bustled into the shop, carrying a tray with a teapot and several covered plates.

"—this time of day," Dot finished, smiling triumphantly.

"I thought you might appreciate another proper cream tea," Elspeth announced. "Can't have you running on empty your second day, can we? I saw you had visitors, so I brought enough for everyone."

"Surveilling the bookstore with opera glasses permanently trained on the front door," Dr. Penrose added dryly.

Elspeth drew herself up with dignity. "I simply like to keep abreast of village happenings. Someone needs to maintain standards."

I managed a smile. "Thank you for the tea, Ms. Willoughby. That's very thoughtful."

"Mrs.," Elspeth corrected. "Widowed these twelve years. And please, it's Elspeth to neighbors." She glanced around the shop with barely concealed curiosity. "I see you're keeping the old arrangements. Very wise. Though perhaps a bit of freshening up wouldn't go amiss. The tourist season will be upon us before we know it."

"I haven't decided on any changes yet," I said diplomatically.

"Of course not, dear. You've only just arrived." Elspeth leaned closer, lowering her voice to a volume that could merely be heard across a small field rather than a large one. "I saw Thornbury leaving in quite a state. You want to watch that one. Always poking about where he's not wanted."

"So I've been told," I said.

"He's been after those old shipping records for years," Dot added.

"For that ridiculous treasure hunt theory," Dr. Penrose scoffed.

"Which may not be entirely ridiculous," Elspeth countered. "My second cousin's brother-in-law was on the council when they dredged the harbor in '97, and he said they found Spanish doubloons, though of course it was all hushed up."

Dr. Penrose rolled his eyes. "Urban legend."

"Rural legend, in this case," Elspeth corrected primly.

The bell jangled yet again, and I suppressed a sigh. At this rate, I'd meet the entire village before lunch.

This time, however, the interruption was more chaotic. Hardy suddenly sprang to life from his spot on the hearth rug, racing toward the door with a series of excited yips. He circled the newcomer's legs, then promptly vomited on the man's well-worn leather boots.

"Oh my god, I'm so sorry!" I gasped, rushing forward with the cloth I'd been using to dust.

The man stared down at the mess, then at Hardy, who wagged his tail guilelessly. "Well," he said in a deep voice tinged with dry amusement, "that's certainly a unique greeting."

I looked up into clear gray-blue eyes that regarded me with a blend of irritation and resignation. The man was tall, with dark hair that curled slightly at the nape of his neck and prematurely silver at the temples.

"I'm mortified," I said, still trying to clean his boots. "He's never done that before."

"Has he been getting into things he shouldn't?" the man asked, his focus shifting to Hardy, who was now sitting innocently as if butter wouldn't melt in his mouth.

"Not that I'm aware of."

"What did you feed him this morning?"

"Just his regular food."

The man crouched down, examining Hardy with careful hands that moved with surprising gentleness. "Has he eaten anything unusual? Old food? Plants? Something from a trash bin?"

"I don't think so, but—" I paused, remembering. "Actually, he did find something in the shop's storage room yesterday. I thought I'd caught him before he ate it, but..."

"What was it?"

"I'm not sure. It looked like old wrapping paper, maybe with food residue?"

The man nodded. "Right. I'm Dr. Elliot Harrington, the local vet. And you'd better bring this little fellow to my clinic this afternoon."

"Is he going to be all right?" I asked, a knot of worry forming in my stomach.

"Probably just mild food poisoning, but I'd like to be sure." Elliot straightened up. "Old buildings like this can have all sorts of nasty things tucked away in corners. Rat poison, mothballs, ancient cleaning products."

"I had no idea," I said, feeling suddenly inadequate. I'd read countless books about living with dogs but hadn't considered the specific hazards of an ancient British bookshop.

"Most pet owners don't," he replied, his tone softening slightly. "My clinic is just outside the village on Mill Road. Can you bring him by after you close?"

"Of course," I said. "And I really am sorry about your boots."

"Occupational hazard," Elliot said with a wry smile. "Though usually I'm safely behind an examination table when it happens." He nodded to the assembled villagers. "Ladies. Dr. Penrose."

As he left, I became aware of the avid interest from my audience.

"Well," Elspeth said, eyebrows raised. "That was rather dramatic."

"Poor little dear," Dot cooed, bending to pet Hardy, who rolled onto his back shamelessly. "Did you eat something nasty?"

"Unhygienic animals," Dr. Penrose muttered. "This is precisely why I prefer books to pets."

"Dr. Harrington is very good with animals," Elspeth informed me. "Divorced, you know. Five years ago. His wife ran off to London with an art dealer. Found village life too provincial, apparently."

"I'm just concerned about my dog," I said firmly.

"Of course, dear," Elspeth patted my arm. "I'm simply providing context."

The parade of visitors continued throughout the afternoon. By closing time, my head was swimming with names, relationships, and village history. I'd learned more about my neighbors' private lives than I'd known about colleagues I'd worked with for years in Charlotte.

Finally alone, I sank into one of the leather armchairs, Austen leaning sympathetically against my leg while Hardy snoozed on the rug, apparently recovered from his earlier indisposition.

"So much for my efficient American management style," I murmured.

The shop creaked in response, the old building settling as the evening cooled. I found myself examining the register once more, tracing my finger over Malcolm's neat entries. R.T. - back room. Tuesday, two weeks ago. Then again the following Thursday. And a final entry the day before my great-aunt's death.

What had Thornbury really been looking for? And why had Malcolm reacted so strongly to his presence?

I closed the ledger and stood, gathering my things. Tomorrow I'd tackle the mysterious archives and see if I could make sense of the Harbormaster's Journal that had everyone so agitated. But first, I needed to get Hardy to his vet appointment and myself back to the cottage for a much-needed glass of wine.

As I locked the shop door, I noticed a small piece of paper tucked into the frame. Unfolding it, I read a single line of spidery handwriting: *You're sitting on a goldmine. Don't be a fool like your aunt.*

Unsigned, but I had little doubt who had left it. I crumpled the note and tossed it into my bag, then whistled for the dogs to follow me across the green toward home.

Behind me, a curtain twitched in the window of Steep & Steep Tea Shop. And in the upstairs storage room of Hampton's Books, a shadow moved briefly across the dust-filled air, though no one was there to cast it.

4

————

I reached the bookshop at 7:30 the next morning, determined to see how Malcolm reacted. If he could be punctual to the point of obsession, I'd find a way to add a little irregularity. The dogs trotted alongside me, their leashes mercifully untangled for once. Hardy seemed fully recovered from yesterday's upset stomach, which Dr. Harrington had diagnosed as a mild reaction to ancient paste from book bindings. "Quite common in old book-shops," he'd explained, his manner warming slightly when I'd demonstrated genuine concern rather than the careless ownership he'd initially suspected.

The morning air held that peculiar English freshness—somehow both crisp and damp simultaneously. A misty drizzle had fallen overnight, leaving the cobblestones slick and the shop windows beaded with moisture. The village green was deserted except for a solitary robin pecking opti-mistically at the wet grass.

As I approached Hampton's Books, something immedi-ately felt wrong. The door stood slightly ajar, a thin sliver of darkness visible between door and frame. I hesitated, checking my watch. Malcolm should have arrived by 7:00, and it was now 7:32.

"Hello?" I called, pushing the door open wider. "Malcolm?"

No answer. Just the groaning of old floorboards and the sense of disturbed air, as if someone had recently passed through.

Austen and Hardy tensed beside me, their usual eager tail-wagging conspicuously absent. Hardy let out a low whine.

I fumbled for the light switch, grateful when the old-fashioned sconces illuminated the main sales floor. Nothing seemed immediately amiss. The cash register stood unopened, the precious tea things remained in their designated spot, and the leather armchairs waited patiently for browsing customers.

"Malcolm?" I called again. "Are you here?"

Only silence answered. Unease prickled along my spine.

I should call someone, I thought, then immediately questioned myself. Call who? The police? Because the door of my own shop was unlocked? Maybe Malcolm had arrived early and stepped out briefly. Maybe I'd failed to lock up properly yesterday. Maybe old buildings in damp climates had doors that spontaneously opened. I was still adjusting to English life; perhaps this was normal.

I unclipped the dogs' leashes, expecting them to trot to their favorite spots. Instead, Austen remained pressed against my leg while Hardy sniffed the air anxiously.

"What is it, guys?" I knelt beside them, suddenly grateful for their company.

A slight breeze whispered through the shop—strange,

since I'd closed the door behind me. Looking up, I noticed papers scattered across the floor near the stairs, as if caught in a draft from above. The staircase led to the fiction section and children's corner on the middle floor, and above that, the storage rooms. The same area where I'd heard noises yesterday.

I gathered the fallen papers—order forms and invoices —and set them on the counter. More papers lay strewn along the staircase, creating a breadcrumb trail I couldn't ignore.

"Hello?" I called up the stairs. "Is anyone there?"

The old wooden steps creaked beneath my weight. Halfway up, I noticed a small dark smudge on the banister. I leaned closer. It looked like... blood? A tiny spot, could be anything really—ink, tea, jam from one of Elspeth's scones.

The dogs refused to follow, stopping at the bottom of the stairs with identical expressions of canine concern.

"Some guard dogs you are," I muttered, continuing upward.

The first floor appeared undisturbed, the fiction shelves standing in orderly rows. But as I crossed toward the back staircase leading to the top floor, I noticed more scattered papers and what looked like scuff marks on the polished wood, as if something heavy had been dragged.

My heart pounded as I climbed the narrow back stairs to the storage level. At the top, I paused, suddenly aware of how alone I was in the shop. The rational part of my brain— the part shaped by corporate meetings and efficiency reports—told me to turn around, go downstairs, and call Malcolm. This was his domain; let him investigate strange noises and open doors.

But the storage room door stood ajar, and beyond it, the

rare book room, with its valuable collection and sturdy lock that Malcolm had emphasized should "never, under any circumstances, be left unlocked."

I inched forward, hearing nothing but my own shallow breathing and the distant sound of Hardy whining below. The storage room looked as if a small tornado had passed through —boxes upended, manuscripts scattered, a chair overturned.

"Hello?" I tried again, my voice embarrassingly faint.

The rare book room lay just beyond, its door not merely unlocked but standing open, the antique lock's keyhole scratched as if someone had tried to force it. I peered around the doorway, then froze.

Dr. Reginald Thornbury lay sprawled across the Oriental carpet, his wire-rimmed glasses askew on his pale face. Beside him, leather-bound manuscripts lay scattered like fallen leaves. His watery blue eyes, which yesterday had regarded me with scholarly disdain, now stared sightlessly at the ceiling. A heavy brass bookend—a Victorian ship in full sail—lay beside his head, flecked with something dark that matched the spreading stain on the carpet.

I'd edited enough crime novels to recognize death when I saw it. My hand flew to my mouth as I stumbled backward, colliding with a stack of boxes that clattered to the floor. For several heartbeats, I simply stood there, breath coming in quick, shallow gasps.

Then training kicked in—not from any crime-solving manual, but from years of corporate crisis management. I backed carefully out of the room, touching nothing, and fumbled for my phone. My trembling fingers dialed 91 before I remembered the right number here was 999.

"Emergency, which service?" asked a calm, professional voice.

"Police," I managed, my own voice sounding distant and strange. "There's been—I think—someone's dead. In my bookshop."

"Can you confirm the address, please?"

I recited the shop's address mechanically, adding, "Hampton's Books, in Tidehaven Cove. I'm the owner. I just found... a body."

"Is the attacker still present?"

"No—I don't think so. I'm alone. Well, except for my dogs downstairs."

"Are you in immediate danger?"

"No, I don't think so. I'm leaving the building now."

"Officers are on their way. Please wait outside for their arrival and don't touch anything further."

I backed carefully down the stairs, keeping my eyes fixed on the upper landing as if expecting the killer to materialize at any moment. Hardy and Austen met me at the bottom, pressing anxiously against my legs.

"Out," I whispered, herding them toward the front door. "We're going outside."

We huddled on the shop's front step, the dogs sensing my distress and staying unusually close. The village was beginning to wake—lights appearing in windows, the distant rumble of a delivery truck. Normal, peaceful morning sounds that now seemed surreal against what I'd just discovered.

My thoughts raced. R.T. That's what had been in the ledger. R.T. - back room - NO. Had Malcolm known this would happen? Had he—

No. I shut down that line of thinking. Malcolm might be stuffy and resistant to change, but he wasn't a murderer. The police would sort this out. This wasn't one of my publishing house's mystery novels; this was real, and I was woefully unqualified to handle it.

I heard rapid footsteps approaching and looked up to see Malcolm hurrying across the green, his bow tie slightly askew as if he'd dressed in haste.

"Miss Hampton?" he called, his normally composed features showing genuine alarm. "What are you doing outside? I just received the most disturbing call from Mrs. Hatchett saying the police are coming to the shop, and I—"

He broke off as he registered my expression. "What on earth has happened?"

"Dr. Thornbury," I said, my voice steadier than I expected. "He's upstairs. In the rare book room. He's dead, Malcolm."

Malcolm's face drained of color. "Dead? But that's—how did he—the rare book room is kept locked at all times!"

"Well, it wasn't locked this morning. And neither was the shop."

His expression shifted from shock to horror to something more complicated. "You think I...?"

"I don't think anything," I said quickly. "But the police will have questions. Lots of questions."

As if summoned by my words, a police car pulled up, its blue light silently rotating. A heavyset man in uniform emerged, followed by a younger officer with a notebook already in hand.

"Miss Hampton?" the older officer asked. "I'm Constable Peters. This is Constable Wilkins. You reported finding a body?"

I nodded, then pointed toward the shop. "Upstairs. Third floor, in the rare book room. It's Dr. Thornbury, a local historian. I think he was... hit with something."

Constable Peters maintained a professionally neutral expression. "And you are the owner of the premises?"

"Yes. I inherited the shop from my great-aunt about a month ago. I only arrived from America last week."

"And this gentleman is...?"

"Malcolm Blackwood," Malcolm supplied. "Assistant manager. I've worked here for thirty years."

The constable nodded. "I'll need both of you to remain here while we secure the scene. Please don't discuss the matter between yourselves for now."

We stood in awkward silence as the officers entered the shop. More police vehicles arrived, along with an unmarked car from which emerged a trim, no-nonsense woman in a well-cut suit.

"Detective Inspector Harriet Drake," she introduced herself crisply. "Devon and Cornwall Police. I understand we have a suspicious death?"

I repeated my explanation, trying to stick to the bare facts. As I spoke, I noticed a small crowd beginning to gather across the green. News traveled fast in village life.

"And when did you last see the deceased alive?" DI Drake asked.

"Yesterday morning. He came to the shop demanding access to some historical manuscripts. He was quite insistent."

"Insistent how?"

I hesitated, aware of Malcolm stiffening beside me. "He claimed my great-aunt had promised him access to something called the Harbormaster's Journal. He was angry when I asked him to wait until I could verify the arrangement."

"And did anyone witness this confrontation?"

"I did," Malcolm interjected. "Dr. Thornbury was most inappropriate in his demands and manner."

DI Drake's gaze shifted to Malcolm. "And you are?"

"Malcolm Blackwood. I've managed the practical operations of Hampton's Books for thirty years. I was present for the... disagreement with Dr. Thornbury."

"I see. And where were you this morning, Mr. Blackwood?"

Malcolm's spine straightened even further. "At home, preparing for work. I always arrive at precisely seven o'clock."

"Except today," the detective noted.

"I received a telephone call from Mrs. Hatchett—she lives above the bakery with a view of the green—telling me there were police vehicles outside the shop. I came immediately."

DI Drake made a noncommittal sound and turned back to me. "Miss Hampton, did you touch anything in the rare book room?"

Why didn't she press for the reason Malcolm was late?

"No. Well, I don't think so. I backed out as soon as I realized what had happened."

"And the shop door was unlocked when you arrived?"

"Yes. It was slightly open, actually."

"Who has keys to the premises?"

"I do, and Malcolm, and..." I paused, realizing I didn't actually know. "Are there others, Malcolm?"

He cleared his throat. "The previous owner—your great-aunt—had a key, naturally. And there's a spare kept in the safe for emergencies."

"We'll need to account for all of them," DI Drake said. "Now, if you'll excuse me, I need to examine the scene."

She disappeared into the shop, leaving us standing

awkwardly under the watchful eyes of a uniformed officer. Across the street, I could see Elspeth peering from her tea shop window, and several other villagers had gathered at a respectful but curious distance.

"This is most distressing," Malcolm murmured, his usual composure noticeably frayed. "Mrs. Hampton-Davies would have been devastated to see the shop associated with such... unpleasantness."

5

Before I could respond, the bell above the shop door jingled, and a thin young man in a rumpled uniform burst out, his face pale. He took one look at the gathering crowd and promptly vomited into the nearest planter.

"First body, Simmons?" Constable Peters called with surprising good humor. The young man nodded miserably and pulled out a handkerchief.

"Forensics are on their way," he reported after composing himself. "Detective Inspector says it looks like blunt force trauma. Preliminary time of death between midnight and four AM."

I felt my own stomach lurch at the casual description. This might be just another dead body to these officers, but to me this was Thornbury, who'd stood in my shop alive and irritated just yesterday.

"Miss Hampton?" Freya's voice cut through my dark thoughts. She stood at the edge of the growing crowd, her eyes wide behind her oversized glasses. "What's happening? Why are there police?"

Malcolm moved as if to intercept her, but the constable held up a hand. "Sorry, sir. No one else enters the scene, and you two stay put for now."

I raised my voice enough for Freya to hear. "There's been an incident. The shop will be closed today."

"An incident?" Freya repeated, pushing her way closer despite the officer's attempt to maintain a perimeter. "What kind of—oh my god, is someone hurt?"

The rumors had clearly not reached her yet. I opened my mouth to reply with some sanitized version of events, but DI Drake reappeared at that moment, her expression grim.

"Miss Hampton, Mr. Blackwood, I'll need formal statements from both of you," she said. "And I'm afraid the shop will remain closed until our investigation is complete."

"How long will that be?" I asked, thinking of the rent due at the end of the month including payroll.

"That depends on what we find." Her gaze was uncomfortably direct. "For now, I need to know exactly who had access to the shop, who knew about your disagreement with Dr. Thornbury, and why a man so desperate to see your rare books was in there after hours."

"I had nothing to do with that," Malcolm said stiffly. "I've always maintained strict security protocols for the rare book room."

"Then perhaps you can explain how someone accessed it without breaking the main door?" DI Drake asked. "And why the lock shows signs of amateur picking rather than professional tools?"

Malcolm's face paled. "I cannot."

"Where do those manuscripts usually live? The ones scattered around the body?"

Malcolm hesitated. "In the glass-fronted case. The one with the specialized humidity controls."

"Which was unlocked," DI Drake noted. "Unlike the other cases."

The implications hung in the air between us. Someone had specifically targeted those particular books—the ones Thornbury had been so eager to see.

Freya had worked her way to the front of the small crowd, her face a picture of distress. "Is it true?" she asked, voice barely above a whisper. "Mrs. Willberry just told me Dr. Thornbury is... dead?"

I nodded grimly.

"Oh my god," Freya gasped. "That's... I just saw him yesterday, outside the shop! He was writing something in that little notebook he always carries."

DI Drake's attention sharpened. "What time was this?"

"Around five? Just before closing," Freya said. "He was standing across the street, watching the shop. I thought it was odd because he usually barges right in when he wants something."

The detective made a note. "Did you mention this to anyone?"

"Just Malcolm, when I got back inside. He said not to worry about it, that Thornbury was just being his usual nuisance self." She glanced apologetically at Malcolm. "Sorry, but that's what you said."

Malcolm's expression had grown increasingly strained. "I may have used those words, yes."

The conversation was interrupted by the arrival of a sleek black BMW that pulled up alongside the police vehicles. The driver's door opened to reveal a tall, elegant woman with blond hair pulled back in a professional chignon. She assessed the scene with sharp green eyes before approaching our small group.

"What's happening here?" she asked, her cultured voice carrying just the right note of concerned curiosity. "Is everyone all right?"

"Police business, ma'am," Constable Peters replied. "I'll have to ask you to step back."

"Of course, officer." She gave him a warm smile. "I'm Victoria Ashford. I've been working with the historical society on the old Tidehaven Manor renovations. I was supposed to meet with Dr. Thornbury this morning about some architectural documentation, but he hasn't answered his phone."

DI Drake looked up from her notes. "You had an appointment with Dr. Thornbury today?"

"Yes, scheduled for nine o'clock at his home." Victoria's gaze traveled to the shop, then back to the detective. "Has something happened to him?"

"I'm afraid Dr. Thornbury has been found deceased," DI Drake said, watching Victoria's reaction carefully.

Victoria's hand flew to her mouth. "Oh no! That's terrible! What happened?"

"We're investigating that now. How well did you know him?"

"Professionally only. He's been helping authenticate some historical documents for the manor renovation. He's rather—was rather—the local expert on Tidehaven Cove's past." She shook her head sadly. "Poor man. He could be difficult, but he was brilliant in his way."

I studied her as she spoke. Victoria Ashford looked like she'd stepped from the pages of Country Life magazine— tailored clothing, understated jewelry, the kind of polished appearance that suggested old money and good taste.

Nothing like the leather-patched, rumpled academic she claimed to have been working with.

"Miss Hampton?" DI Drake's voice pulled me from my observations. "I'd like you to come to the station now to give your statement."

"Of course," I agreed.

"What about the dogs?" I gestured to Austen and Hardy, who had been sitting remarkably quietly throughout the chaos.

"Take them with you for now," she advised. "You won't be returning to the shop today."

As if to emphasize her point, more police personnel arrived, including a van marked "Forensic Services." Yellow crime scene tape was being strung across the shop door. The sight was so incongruous—that cheerful yellow plastic defacing the dignified old bookshop—that I felt a sudden, absurd urge to laugh.

"You can't just handle the rare books," Malcolm protested. "You'll damage them. Some of them are valuable."

DI Drake looked to the head of the forensic team who assured us he knew how to handle precious items.

"MISS HAMPTON?" Malcolm's voice was low and strained. "I want you to know that I had nothing to do with this. Nothing whatsoever."

I looked at him—really looked—and saw the genuine distress behind his proper facade. Whatever our differences, whatever his secrets, I didn't believe Malcolm Blackwood was a murderer.

"I know," I said simply.

"The Harbormaster's Journal," he said urgently as an

officer approached to escort me to a waiting police car. "Check if it's missing. That's what he was after."

Before I could ask what he meant, DI Drake called for Malcolm to accompany another officer, and we were separated.

I gathered the dogs' leashes and followed the constable to the car, feeling the weight of curious stares from the assembled villagers. In the space of twenty-four hours, I'd gone from being the slightly eccentric American newcomer to the central figure in a murder investigation.

As the police car pulled away, I caught a glimpse of Victoria Ashford watching us leave, her expression unreadable. Behind her, the bookshop stood wrapped in police tape, its windows like sad eyes witnessing the unfolding tragedy.

Less than a week in England, and I'd already found myself at the center of a very British murder. Somehow, I didn't think this was what my great-aunt had intended when she left me her legacy.

6

The station was exactly as I'd imagined a small British police facility would be—a peculiar blend of modern technology awkwardly housed in a building that had probably witnessed the coronation of Queen Victoria. Dingy fluorescent lighting did no favors for the institutional green walls, and the hard plastic chair beneath me seemed designed by someone with a thorough knowledge of human discomfort.

Austen sat primly at my feet while Hardy kept glancing in the direction of the young desk sergeant, who'd passed him biscuit bits when he thought no one was looking.

"More tea, Miss Hampton?" Detective Inspector Drake pushed a chipped mug across the interview room table.

"No, thank you." I'd already consumed two cups during the hour I'd spent recounting every detail of my brief acquaintance with Reginald Thornbury.

"Let's go over this one more time," she said, consulting her notes. "You arrived in England six days ago. You took possession of Hampton's Books three days ago. Yesterday, Thornbury came to the shop demanding access to rare manuscripts, claiming your great-aunt had granted permission."

"That's right."

"You denied him access."

"I asked him to come back next week, when I'd had time to verify his claims."

"And he threatened you."

I shifted uncomfortably. "Not physically. He said I'd 'regret not cooperating.' I took it as academic bluster."

DI Drake's expression remained neutral. "This morning, you arrived to find the shop unlocked, papers scattered, and Dr. Thornbury dead in the rare book room."

"Yes."

"A room that Malcolm Blackwood claims is kept 'securely locked at all times.'"

"That's what he told me." I knew better than to say yes, because they weren't my words, and any slight error could look bad for me or Malcolm.

"Yet someone accessed it without forcing the main door to the shop." She leaned forward slightly. "Miss Hampton, who would benefit from Dr. Thornbury's death?"

The question hung between us. I'd been expecting it, of course—I'd edited enough mysteries to recognize the standard investigative path—but having it directed at me felt surreal.

"I hardly knew the man," I said. "I can't imagine who would want him dead."

"Let me help you imagine," DI Drake replied. "Perhaps someone who had just inherited a valuable collection of rare books and didn't want Thornbury examining them too closely? Someone who stood to lose if certain 'manuscripts' turned out to be historically significant beyond their monetary value?"

My mouth fell open. "You think I killed him? That's absurd! I just arrived in the country!"

"Making you the perfect suspect, some might say. No history, no known connection to the victim, inheriting valuable property with potential hidden treasures."

"I'm an editor, not a murderer!" My voice rose despite my best efforts. "I publish books, I don't kill people over them!"

DI Drake sat back, expression unchanged. "Former editor. Currently a bookshop owner with a dead academic in her rare book room. An academic who, by multiple accounts, was quite interested in specific materials in your possession."

I took a deep breath, reminding myself that this was just procedure. They had to consider every angle, every suspect. Even ridiculous ones.

"Detective Inspector, I understand you're doing your job. But think about this logically. I arrived in England less than a week ago. I barely knew what was in that rare book room. According to your timeline, Thornbury was killed sometime after midnight. I was at home, in bed."

"Can anyone verify that?"

"Just my dogs." I gestured to Austen and Hardy. "And I doubt their testimony would hold up in court."

For the first time, something like amusement flickered across the detective's face. "No, I don't imagine it would." She made another note before continuing. "Tell me about your relationship with Malcolm Blackwood."

"There isn't one. He worked for my great-aunt for thirty years. We met four days ago."

"And how would you characterize your interactions?"

I chose my words carefully. "Professional, if a bit strained. He's... resistant to change, and I represent a lot of change."

"Would you say he was protective of the shop? Of its contents?"

"Extremely." I remembered his reaction to Thornbury. "Particularly the rare books."

"And how did he react to Thornbury's visit yesterday?"

"He was angry. More than I would have expected for a simple business dispute."

"Angry enough to kill?"

The question shocked me, though I should have seen it coming. "I don't know Malcolm well enough to judge that, but no, I wouldn't think so. He's proper to the point of rigidity."

"Rigid people sometimes snap, Miss Hampton." She closed her notebook. "What do you know about the Harbormaster's Journal?"

The abrupt shift caught me off guard. "Almost nothing. Thornbury wanted to see it. Malcolm mentioned it was connected to some shipwreck. The Maria Constance, I think he called it."

"The Maria Constance," DI Drake repeated. "A merchant vessel that sank off the Devon coast in 1843, reportedly carrying a substantial cargo of gold and antiquities. Its exact location has been sought by treasure hunters for generations."

"And Thornbury thought this journal contained clues to its location?"

"So it would seem. Our officers found his notebook at the scene, filled with research notes about the shipwreck and multiple references to 'H.J.' and 'Hampton's.'"

I felt a chill that had nothing to do with the room's temperature. "And is the journal missing?"

DI Drake's gaze sharpened. "Why do you ask that?"

"Malcolm mentioned it, just before we were separated.

He said to check if it was missing, that it was what Thornbury was after."

"Interesting that his concern was for the journal, not the man found dead beside it." She made another note. "We're still cataloging what was taken. Do you have any documentation of what should be in that collection?"

I shook my head. "Not that I've found yet. Malcolm might know."

"Yes, Mr. Blackwood seems to know rather a lot about the shop's contents." She stood. "You're free to go for now, Miss Hampton, but don't leave the area. We'll need to speak with you again."

"Am I a suspect?" I asked bluntly.

"Everyone connected to the shop is of interest to our investigation," she replied, not quite answering my question. "Where will you be staying? The shop is a crime scene and will remain closed for at least several days."

"My home on Cottage Lane." I gathered the dogs' leashes. "When can I reopen the shop?"

"That depends on how quickly we process the scene and what we find. I'd estimate a minimum of three days, possibly longer."

Three days without income from a business that was already struggling. Perfect.

As I was led back to the reception area, I found Malcolm sitting stiffly on a bench, his bow tie slightly askew. He looked up as I approached, his expression drawn.

"Miss Hampton," he acknowledged with a short nod. "I trust you were treated appropriately?"

"As well as can be expected when you're suspected of murder," I replied.

His eyebrows rose slightly. "They can't seriously believe you had anything to do with this."

"I'm not sure what they believe, but they certainly asked a lot of questions about my inheritance and the timing of my arrival."

Malcolm made a disapproving sound. "Preposterous. You barely knew the man."

"Neither did you, apparently," I countered. "Yet you seemed to have quite a strong reaction to him yesterday."

A flicker of something—guilt? fear? crossed his face. "Thornbury and I had... professional disagreements over the years. Nothing more."

Before I could press further, a constable called Malcolm's name, summoning him to his own interview.

"Miss Hampton," he said quietly as he stood, "be careful what you say about the journal. Not everyone understands its significance."

With that cryptic warning, he followed the officer down the corridor, leaving me with more questions than answers.

Outside the station, I found Freya pacing nervously on the sidewalk. Her usual exuberance had been replaced by wide-eyed anxiety, and several pencils had escaped her haphazard bun.

"Ginny!" she exclaimed when she saw me. "Are you all right? They wouldn't tell me anything, just that the shop was closed and I should go home, but Mrs. Willberry said Dr. Thornbury was dead, and then someone said it might be murder, and I didn't know what to think!"

She delivered this without taking a breath, reminding me of our first meeting.

"Slow down, Freya. Yes, Dr. Thornbury is dead. Yes, the police think it's murder. And yes, the shop is closed for now."

"But what happened? Who would kill him?"

"That's what the police are trying to figure out." I started walking, needing to move after hours of sitting in the interview room. Freya fell into step beside me, while the dogs trotted ahead, seemingly delighted by this unexpected daytime outing.

"Do they think it was a robbery?" she asked, lowering her voice despite the empty street. "The rare books are quite valuable. Malcolm always said they were worth more than the rest of the shop combined."

7

I considered how much to share. Freya was technically my employee, but she'd also been at the shop far longer than I had.

"Did you know about something called the Harbormaster's Journal?" I asked finally.

Freya's eyes widened. "The journal? It's real? I thought it was just a local legend, like the treasure ship."

"The Maria Constance?"

She nodded eagerly. "It's a famous story around here. A merchant vessel that sank in a storm, carrying gold from the colonies. People have been searching for it for centuries. Some say the ship's captain survived and recorded the coordinates in his private journal, which eventually found its way to a local collection." She paused. "Are you saying your great-aunt had it all this time?"

"I don't know what she had," I admitted. "But Thornbury seemed to think the journal was in our rare book room, and now he's dead."

"Oh my god," Freya breathed. "That's... that's like something from a novel!"

"Unfortunately, real murder is a lot messier and more inconvenient than fictional murder," I said dryly. "The shop is closed for the foreseeable future."

Her face fell. "So I'm out of a job? Just like that?"

I hadn't even considered my employees would worry about that. "No, of course not. You're still employed. I'll figure something out."

"Really? Because I really need the hours. My dissertation expenses are—"

"Freya," I cut in, "I promise you're not losing your job. But I need to figure out what we can do while the shop is closed."

She visibly relaxed. "Thank you. I could help with inventory or cleaning or whatever needs doing when they let us back in. I'm good with organization, despite appearances." She gestured to her haphazard outfit and the pencil now dangling precariously from her hair.

We had reached the village green, and I paused, reluctant to return to my empty cottage with nothing but my thoughts and suspicions for company.

"Fancy a cup of tea?" Freya suggested, reading my hesitation. "Elspeth's shop is just there, and she makes the best scones in Devon. Well, that's what she says, anyway."

The thought of facing Elspeth's interrogation made me wince, but I was hungry, and the cottage's kitchen remained a mysterious territory I'd barely begun to navigate.

"Lead the way," I agreed.

Inside, Steep & Steep Tea Shop was exactly what I'd expect from a quintessential English tearoom—floral tablecloths, mismatched vintage china, and the comforting aroma of baked goods and brewed tea. At eleven on a weekday morning, it was nearly empty, with just a couple of elderly ladies in one corner.

The bell above the door announced our arrival, and Elspeth emerged from the back room with the speed of someone who'd been waiting for precisely this moment.

"My dear!" she exclaimed, bustling over. "What a dreadful business! Absolutely dreadful! Are you quite all right? You must be in shock. Sit down immediately, I'll bring you my special calming blend. Rose hip and chamomile, excellent for trauma."

She steered me to a table by the window—with an excellent view of the bookshop across the green, I noted—and disappeared before I could respond.

"Brace yourself," Freya murmured as we sat. "She's been beside herself with excitement all morning. First murder in Tidehaven Cove since 1986, apparently."

"Wonderful," I muttered. "I've provided the village entertainment for the month."

"Oh, much longer than that," Freya assured me. "Mrs. Peterson's scandalous conservatory extension was the talk of the village for nearly six months, and nobody even died."

Elspeth reappeared with a tray laden with teapot, cups, and a towering plate of scones. "On the house, dear. After what you've been through!" She set everything down and pulled up a chair uninvited. "Now, tell me everything. Was it truly dreadful? Did you actually find the body? They're saying it was that brass bookend from the Harrington collection—the ship in full sail? Always thought it looked dangerous myself, all those pointy masts."

I blinked at the barrage. "I'm sorry, Elspeth, but the police have asked me not to discuss the details."

"Of course, of course." She leaned closer. "But just between us, was there much blood? Only Mrs. Hatchett said she saw the medical examiner's van, and they only bring that for the really gruesome ones."

"Elspeth," I said firmly, "I really can't discuss it."

She looked disappointed but rallied quickly. "Well, naturally, you must be in shock. Drink your tea, dear. And you might want to know that Oliver Blackthorn has been telling anyone who'll listen that the shop will surely be sold now. 'No American girl is going to stay after this,' were his exact words, according to my customer from the post office."

My hands tightened around the teacup. "Is that so?"

"Oh yes. He seemed quite certain. Already talking about expansion plans, if you can believe it! The nerve of the man, with poor Dr. Thornbury hardly cold."

Freya shot me a concerned look. "Ginny isn't selling the shop."

"Of course not," I agreed, though the thought had flashed through my mind during my darkest moments at the police station. What had I gotten myself into? A struggling business, a hostile employee, and now a murder. But something in Oliver's certainty rankled. "Mr. Blackthorn will be disappointed."

"And that Victoria Ashford's been asking questions too," Elspeth continued, lowering her voice. "She was in here earlier, wanting to know all about you and the shop. Very interested in the building's history. Said she was working with the historical society, but if you ask me, developers stick together."

"Victoria Ashford?" I recalled the polished blond woman outside the bookshop. "What did she want to know?"

"Everything! When you arrived, how well you knew your great-aunt, whether you'd mentioned selling. Most curious about the building itself—asking about original features, architectural details, that sort of thing." Elspeth sniffed disapprovingly. "I told her the shop's been a Hampton family business for generations and wasn't likely to change hands. That silenced her."

I filed away this information. Victoria's interest seemed excessive for someone who'd just happened upon a crime scene.

"Did she mention knowing Dr. Thornbury?" I asked casually.

"Said they were working together on some historical documentation project. Though that's the first I've heard of it, and I know everything that happens in this village." Elspeth poured more tea with the precision of someone who could do it blindfolded. "Thornbury wasn't one to share credit, especially with a woman from London."

"She's from London?" Freya asked.

"Supposedly," Elspeth replied. "Bought the old Tide-haven Manor six months ago. Plans to 'restore it to its former glory,' whatever that means. Probably turning it into holiday flats. They all do."

The bell jingled, announcing new customers, and Elspeth reluctantly excused herself, but not before promising to return with "just a few more details you might find interesting."

"She knows everything," Freya said once Elspeth was out of earshot. "It's terrifying and useful in equal measure."

I nibbled a scone, which was indeed excellent. "How long have you worked at the shop, Freya?"

"Almost two years. I started just after I began my master's program. The hours fit perfectly around my classes, and your great-aunt was wonderful about letting me study during quiet periods."

"Did you know her well?"

Freya considered this. "Not in a personal way. She was rather private. But she was kind, in her own reserved manner. She loved that shop more than anything." She hesitated. "That's why it was so strange when she started letting Thornbury examine the rare books. It happened about three months before she died."

I set down my teacup. "What do you mean?"

"Well, she'd always been super protective of the rare book room. Malcolm had to practically perform a security ritual just to dust in there. But suddenly, Thornbury was being allowed private sessions with certain manuscripts. Malcolm was furious about it, but your great-aunt insisted."

"When exactly was this?"

"February, I think? She complained about feeling ill in March and passed away in April." Freya twisted a strand of hair nervously. "Don't tell Malcolm I told you. He gets weird about anything involving your great-aunt's final months."

"Why would that be?"

Freya leaned forward. "I think they argued. I came in early one morning and heard them in the rare book room. Your great-aunt said something about 'the truth being more important than pride,' and Malcolm stormed out looking like thunder. They were perfectly civil afterward, but something had changed."

I digested this information along with my scone. What truth had my great-aunt been referring to? And why had she suddenly granted Thornbury access after years of refusal?

"Freya, have you ever seen the Harbormaster's Journal?"

She frowned in concentration. "No, but there was a leather document case your great-aunt kept in her private desk upstairs—not in the rare book room proper. She took it out a few times when Thornbury visited. Old-fashioned, with brass corners and a wax seal on the front."

"And would Malcolm have known about this?"

"Oh, definitely. He knows where every book and paper in

that shop belongs." She paused. "Do you think that's what Thornbury was after when he was killed?"

"I think it's a possibility the police are considering," I said carefully. It did seem odd that if Malcolm knew where every book in the shop lived, this journal seemed to be hard to find.

"But why kill him? Why not just steal it?"

It was a good question, and one I didn't have an answer for.

Our conversation was interrupted by the shop bell again. This time, Dot bustled in, spotted me, and made a beeline for our table.

"There you are, dear! I've been looking everywhere! Are you all right? What a dreadful shock for you!" She pulled up a chair without waiting for an invitation. "I've made a shepherd's pie—my mother's recipe, very comforting in times of crisis. It's waiting at your cottage. The police wouldn't let me deliver it earlier."

"That's very kind, Dot," I said, genuinely touched.

"Least I could do. Neighbors look after each other." She glanced around and lowered her voice. "Is it true they suspect Malcolm? Only Dr. Penrose said he saw him coming from the direction of the bookshop very early this morning, well before his usual time."

I stared at her. "What? When was this?"

"Around six, he said. Penrose is an insomniac, up at all hours. Said he noticed because it was unusual."

My mind raced. Malcolm had told the police he was at home until he received the call about police at the bookshop. If Penrose had seen him earlier...

"I'm sure there's an explanation," I said, unwilling to fuel speculation, especially given my own suspicions.

"Of course, dear," Dot agreed, though her expression

suggested otherwise. "Malcolm's been devoted to that shop for decades. Mind you, he and Thornbury did have that terrible row at the historical society meeting last month. Something about authentication of documents. Nearly came to blows, according to Reverend Williams."

The revelations were coming too fast. Malcolm and Thornbury had a public argument recently? Why hadn't Malcolm mentioned this?

"I should get back to my cottage," I said, suddenly exhausted. "It's been a long morning."

"Of course, dear. You need rest after such a shock." Dot patted my hand. "Though you might want to take the back path. There are reporters by the green—local paper and someone from a Plymouth station. News travels fast."

Perfect. Journalists were the last thing I needed right now.

I thanked Elspeth for the tea and scones, extracted a promise from Freya to meet tomorrow to discuss alternative work arrangements, and headed out through the tea shop's back door with Dot's detailed instructions on how to avoid the main roads.

As I walked the narrow alley that would eventually connect to Cottage Lane, my mind sifted through the day's revelations. Malcolm having a public argument with Thornbury. My great-aunt granting Thornbury access to precious documents after years of refusal. Victoria Ashford asking questions about the shop and its history. The mysterious Harbormaster's Journal that might lead to sunken treasure.

And somewhere in this tangle of history, ambition, and secrecy, a killer had decided Reginald Thornbury needed to die.

I rounded the corner onto Cottage Lane and stopped

short. A familiar figure stood at my garden gate—the last person I expected or wanted to see.

Dr. Elliot Harrington turned as I approached, his expression unreadable. "Miss Hampton," he greeted me formally. "I heard about what happened. I thought you might need some help with the dogs, given the circumstances."

Hardy strained toward him excitedly, apparently having forgiven or forgotten yesterday's undignified examination.

"That's... thoughtful," I managed, caught off guard by his unexpected concern. "But we're fine."

"Are you?" His direct gaze was disconcerting. "Finding a murdered man in your shop isn't what most people would define as 'fine.'"

Put that way, he had a point.

"The dogs could probably use a proper walk," I conceded. "It's been a stressful morning for all of us."

"I know a good path along the stream," he offered. "Far from curious villagers and their questions."

The promise of escape from prying eyes was tempting. And despite his initially cool manner yesterday, something about Elliot Harrington's calm presence felt reassuring on this most unsettling of days.

"Let me just drop off my bag," I said, unlocking the cottage door.

As I stepped inside, a thought struck me. Elliot was one of the few people in the village who likely had no connection to Thornbury, the bookshop, or whatever historical intrigue surrounded the Harbormaster's Journal. An outsider's perspective might be exactly what I needed.

"Actually," I called back to him, "do you have time for tea? I could use a sounding board."

He hesitated, then nodded. "I've rescheduled my morning appointments. My time is yours."

Not the most effusive acceptance, but I'd take it. After all, people had been murdered for less than refusing a British person's offer of tea.

And perhaps, between the village gossip and police suspicions, what I needed most was someone with no stake in Tidehaven Cove's secrets—someone who might help me separate fact from fiction before I found myself too deeply entangled in both.

8

"I'm a terrible hostess," I admitted, surveying my kitchen with fresh eyes as Elliot entered. Unpacked boxes lined one wall, the countertops bore a forensic trail of hasty breakfasts, and I realized with horror that a pair of dog-chewed slippers lay abandoned by the Aga. "I haven't really settled in yet."

"No need to apologize," Elliot replied, seeming genuinely unbothered as he bent to greet the dogs. "I imagine finding a body in your bookshop has somewhat disrupted your unpacking schedule."

He said this so matter-of-factly that I couldn't help but smile. Everyone else had been either morbidly fascinated or performatively horrified by the morning's events. Elliot's straightforward acknowledgment was oddly refreshing.

"You could say that." I filled the kettle and placed it on the Aga's hotplate, still uncertain exactly how the temperamental beast regulated its heat. "Though it appears my reputation in the village is now permanently established. The American who brought murder to Tidehaven Cove."

"Hardly your fault," Elliot said, leaning against the doorframe. Standing in my kitchen, he seemed larger somehow, his tall frame making the room feel smaller. "Tidehaven Cove has a long history of dramatic events despite its sleepy appearance. You're simply the latest chapter."

I raised an eyebrow. "You sound remarkably unconcerned about murder in your village."

"I'm a veterinarian. I deal with life and death daily." He crossed to the window, looking out at the garden. "And having grown up nearby, I'm well acquainted with the village's tendency to dramatize. By next week, the story will involve ancient curses and ghostly sightings."

"It already does," I snorted. "Malcolm's been feeding me stories about the shop ghost since I arrived."

Elliot turned, curiosity flickering in his eyes. "Ghost stories? From Malcolm Blackwood? The man who corrects people's pronunciation of 'scone' and leaves passive-aggressive notes about proper bookmark usage?"

"The very same." I searched through cabinets for teacups that matched. "Did you know Malcolm well? Before all this, I mean."

"Not socially. He brings in the bookshop's cat for checkups." Elliot paused. "Wait—you haven't mentioned the cat. Is he...?"

"There's a bookshop cat?" This was news to me. "I haven't seen one."

"Captain typically lives upstairs. He's part stray but seems to have adopted the bookshop as his base." Elliot frowned. "You should check on him when you're allowed back in. He might be distressed."

I felt a stab of guilt. Four days at the shop, and I hadn't even realized there was a resident cat. What else had I missed?

The kettle began to whistle, rescuing me from my

thoughts. I prepared the tea with more confidence than I felt, aware of Elliot's quiet observation.

"Why did you really come by?" I asked, setting a steaming mug before him. "It wasn't just about the dogs."

He accepted the tea with a nod of thanks. "Directness. How refreshing."

"I've had a morning of police interrogation and village speculation. I think I've reached my quota for polite evasion."

"Fair enough." He took a sip before answering. "I came because I overheard Victoria Ashford asking questions about you at the manor site this morning. Quite detailed questions. I thought you should know."

My hand stilled around my mug. "What kind of questions?"

"How long you'd been here, your background, whether you planned to stay in Tidehaven Cove. She seemed particularly interested in your relationship with your great-aunt."

So not only at the tea shop? "Did she mention the murder?"

"Only to express shock and offer her assistance with the investigation. Said she had 'expertise in historical property crimes' that might prove useful." Elliot's expression remained neutral, but I caught the slight skepticism in his tone.

"You don't believe her?"

"I make it a policy not to trust people who use tragedies as networking opportunities."

I couldn't argue with that logic. "She told the police she had an appointment with Thornbury this morning—something about architectural documentation."

"Possible," Elliot conceded. "Thornbury positioned

himself as the local expert on anything historical, despite his questionable academic credentials."

"You knew him?"

"By reputation mostly. He tried to authenticate some veterinary texts I inherited from my grandfather. Declared them 'obviously Victorian reproductions' and offered fifty pounds for the lot." A ghost of a smile touched his lips. "They were actually rare eighteenth-century first editions worth considerably more."

"So he wasn't above a bit of deception for personal gain?"

"That would be stating it mildly." Elliot set his mug down. "Is that why you invited me in? To question me about Thornbury?"

I felt heat rise to my cheeks. "Not entirely. I thought... I could use someone to talk to who isn't either suspecting me of murder or pumping me for gossip."

"And you chose the village vet? The man whose boots your dog vomited on yesterday?"

Put that way, it did seem an odd choice.

"You're right, I'm sorry. It's inappropriate to involve you in this." I stood, prepared to show him out.

"I didn't say I was unwilling." Elliot remained seated, studying me with those disconcertingly direct eyes. "Just curious about your reasoning."

I sank back down. "You're not embedded in village politics. You're educated enough to understand the historical elements. And you seem..." I searched for the right word. "Reliable."

"High praise indeed." His dry tone couldn't quite hide what might have been amusement. "Very well. Tell me what's troubling you, beyond the obvious dead body."

I took a deep breath and outlined the morning's events, from finding Thornbury to my interview with DI Drake. I explained about the Harbormaster's Journal and the connection to the Maria Constance shipwreck. I described Malcolm's suspicious behavior and Victoria Ashford's convenient appearance.

Elliot listened without interruption, his expression thoughtful. When I finished, he remained silent for a long moment.

"You realize," he finally said, "that you're describing a classic treasure hunt murder."

"I'm aware it sounds like fiction," I admitted. "But Thornbury is genuinely dead, and now the police are treating me like a suspect."

"Not you specifically," Elliot clarified. "Anyone connected to the bookshop. It's standard procedure."

"Speaking from experience, Doctor?"

"Veterinary school involved more post-mortems than you might expect." He leaned forward. "The journal, has anyone confirmed whether it's missing?"

"The police were cataloging everything when I left. But Malcolm seemed convinced it was what Thornbury was after."

"And you trust Malcolm's assessment?"

I hesitated. "I don't know. Yesterday I would have said he's just a slightly stuffy bookseller. Now I find out he had a public argument with the victim recently, may have been seen near the shop around the time of the murder, and has been keeping secrets about my great-aunt's final months."

"All concerning, certainly." Elliot paused, then asked, "What do you know about your great-aunt's passing?"

"Not much. She started to feel ill in late March and died two weeks later. The solicitor said it was heart failure."

"It was," Elliot confirmed. "I knew her, slightly. We attended all the fairs and community events. Lots of that kind of relationships in the village. She mentioned you sometimes."

This surprised me. "She did?"

"Said her American grand-niece had more sense about books than most of the literary crowd in London. High praise from Vivian. She wasn't generous with compliments."

A warm feeling spread through me. I'd exchanged letters with Great-Aunt Vivian for years, bonding over our shared love of literature, but I'd never been sure how she spoke of me to others.

"Did she ever mention health concerns? Or feeling threatened?"

Elliot's brow furrowed. "Threatened? No. But then, I was the cat's doctor, not hers."

"It just seems strange—she grants Thornbury access to rare documents after years of refusal, argues with Malcolm about 'truth being more important than pride,' and then conveniently dies, leaving everything to a relative an ocean away."

"You think her death wasn't natural?" Elliot looked genuinely concerned now.

"I don't know what to think. But too many things don't add up." I wrapped my hands around my mug, drawing comfort from its warmth. "Why would someone kill Thornbury in the shop? Why not just steal whatever they were after? And why now, with me newly arrived?"

"Perhaps your arrival accelerated someone's timetable," Elliot suggested. "If they feared you might discover something your great-aunt had hidden."

The thought sent a chill through me. "But what? And hidden where? I've barely scratched the surface of the shop's inventory."

"Start with what you know Thornbury wanted this

Harbormaster's Journal. If it exists and contains what legend claims, it could be worth killing for."

"A map to sunken treasure? It sounds absurd."

"People have killed for less," Elliot said simply. "And the Maria Constance isn't just any shipwreck. It's deeply embedded in local mythology. There are families around here who've spent generations searching."

I thought of Malcolm's vehemence about keeping Thornbury away from the archives. "So if someone believed they'd finally located the journal..."

"They might take extreme measures to acquire it." Elliot glanced at his watch. "I should go. I've rescheduled patients, not canceled them entirely."

As he stood, Hardy trotted over with his leash in his mouth, looking expectantly between us.

"Sorry, fellow," Elliot told him. "Rain check on that walk."

"Thank you," I said, following him to the door. "For coming by, I mean. And for listening."

He paused on the threshold. "Be careful, Miss Hampton. Treasure hunters can be dangerous enough. Murderous ones more so."

"Ginny," I corrected. "If we're going to discuss murder and mayhem, you might as well use my first name."

An almost-smile tugged at his mouth. "Ginny, then." He stepped outside, then turned back. "One more thing—check your great-aunt's personal papers if you can. People facing mortality often leave records of the things that concern them."

With that practical advice, he strode away, his tall figure quickly disappearing around the bend in the lane.

I closed the door, my mind racing with new possibilities. Great-Aunt Vivian's personal papers—where would those be? Not at the shop; the police had that locked down. But perhaps here, in the cottage I'd inherited alongside the bookshop?

The thought had barely formed when a sharp knock jolted me back to reality. Expecting Elliot had returned, I swung the door open with less caution than was perhaps wise on the day a murderer had visited my shop.

Instead of the veterinarian, I found myself face to face with Victoria Ashford.

9

"Miss Hampton," she greeted me with a sympathetic smile that didn't quite reach her eyes. "I hope I'm not intruding. I wanted to check how you're doing after this morning's dreadful discovery."

Up close, she was even more polished than I'd initially thought—cashmere sweater, pearls, and the kind of expertly applied makeup that suggests wealth rather than vanity. A silver charm bracelet caught the light as she extended her hand.

"Ms. Ashford," I acknowledged, not inviting her in. "That's very thoughtful, but I'm actually quite busy."

"Of course, of course." She didn't withdraw. "I just wanted to express my condolences and offer my assistance. As I mentioned to the police, I was working with Dr. Thornbury on historical documentation for Tidehaven Manor."

"So I heard. What exactly were you documenting?"

If my direct question surprised her, she didn't show it. "Architectural provenance, primarily. The manor has had several renovations over the centuries, not all of them properly recorded. Reginald—Dr. Thornbury—was helping establish its original features."

The explanation sounded plausible, but something in her too-perfect composure made me uneasy.

"And that required accessing historical ship records?" I asked innocently.

A flicker—so brief I almost missed it—crossed her face. "Ship records? I'm not sure what you mean."

"Dr. Thornbury seemed quite interested in maritime history. Specifically, documents that might be in my shop's archive."

"Ah." Her smile returned. "Reginald had many research interests. I couldn't possibly keep track of them all. Our focus was strictly architectural." She glanced past me into the cottage. "What a charming place. Original seventeenth-century construction, yes? Those ceiling beams are exquisite."

Her attempt to change the subject was as transparent as it was effective. I found myself unwillingly following her gaze upward.

"I wouldn't know. I've only been here a week."

"Of course. Such a tragedy to have your new beginning marred by this awful event." She reached out as if to pat my arm, then seemed to think better of it. "If you'd like any advice about the property or the shop building—from a preservation perspective—I'd be happy to help. These old structures can be so challenging to maintain."

"Thank you, but I think I'll manage."

"Certainly. But should you decide the responsibilities of two historical properties are too much..." She produced a business card from her pocket. "Ashford Heritage Developments specializes in sensitive renovation of significant buildings. We'd ensure your great-aunt's legacy remained intact, whatever you decided."

I took the card automatically. "Are you offering to buy my properties, Ms. Ashford?"

Her laugh was practiced and musical. "Not at all! Just offering my professional services. Though should you ever consider selling, I'd be delighted to discuss options that would honor the historical significance."

"I'll keep that in mind," I said, making no effort to hide my skepticism.

"Please do." She stepped back, apparently sensing she'd pushed as far as she could. "And if you remember anything about Dr. Thornbury's research that might help the police, do let me know. We were working quite closely."

She turned to leave, then paused. "I heard Dr. Harrington was here earlier. Such a dedicated veterinarian. The entire village relies on him, though he keeps to himself socially. Divorced, you know. Rather messily."

The information was delivered with such casual precision that I almost missed the intent behind it. Almost.

"I value professional relationships," I replied blandly. "Good day, Ms. Ashford."

I closed the door before she could respond, then stood for a moment, processing the encounter. Why was Victoria Ashford really interested in my properties? And why mention Elliot's divorce?

I glanced at her business card—cream-colored, expensive stock, embossed with a stylized 'A' above "Ashford Heritage Developments" and the tagline "Preserving the Past, Securing the Future." Her mobile number was handwritten on the back, alongside the words "Call anytime. Happy to help."

I set it aside with a mental note to look up her company

later. For now, I had more pressing concerns, starting with my great-aunt's personal papers.

The cottage had come fully furnished, with much of Great-Aunt Vivian's belongings still in place. I'd been sleeping in the guest room, reluctant to disturb the master bedroom that still held her clothes and personal items. Now, I headed upstairs with purpose, the dogs following curiously.

The master bedroom was exactly as I'd left it—slightly musty, with heavy floral curtains filtering the midday light. A carved mahogany wardrobe dominated one wall, while a matching dressing table stood beneath the window. Beside the neatly made bed, a small writing desk held a stack of leather-bound volumes—journals, perhaps?

I sat at the desk and opened the top volume. It was indeed a journal, my great-aunt's elegant handwriting filling the pages with observations about village life, the book-shop's daily business, and occasional literary reflections. I checked the date—2018. Too early.

The next journal covered 2019, and the third began January 2020. I flipped to March, where the entries became increasingly irregular, likely as her health declined.

March 15, 2020: *R.T. came again today. His persistence is remarkable, if unwelcome. M. believes I should continue to refuse, but I'm beginning to wonder if the truth might be better served by transparency. Some secrets have been kept too long.*

My pulse quickened. R.T.—Reginald Thornbury. And M. could only be Malcolm.

March 20: *Made the decision today. M. will be furious, but the journal belongs to history, not to any one family. R.T. will be granted access under strict supervision. I only hope I'm doing the right thing.*

March 27: *Shocking revelations from the journal. If R.T. is correct about the coordinates, everything changes. M. refuses to believe it, says R.T. is manipulating historical facts for personal gain. Perhaps, but the evidence is compelling. I've made copies of the relevant pages as insurance.*

Insurance against what? Or whom?

April 3: *My health continues to deteriorate. M. blames stress from the R.T. situation and the isolation orders, but I fear it's simply time catching up with me. Have written to G. again. She, at least, will approach the situation with fresh eyes, unburdened by old loyalties and village politics.*

G. That was me—Ginny. She'd been writing to me about Thornbury?

I frantically searched my memory. Her last letter had arrived in February, full of her usual observations about books and village characters. Nothing about historical journals or treasure maps. Had she sent another letter that never arrived?

The final entry was dated April 10, just five days before her death.

Have made the necessary arrangements. The journal will be secured until G. arrives. M. disapproves, but it's no longer his decision to make. The truth changes everything about the shipwreck, and the families deserve to know, whatever the consequences for old reputations.

I sat back, mind spinning. My great-aunt had granted Thornbury access to the journal against Malcolm's wishes. She'd discovered something shocking about the shipwreck —something that affected "old reputations." She'd made copies of key pages as "insurance." And she'd apparently tried to tell me about it.

But what had she found? And where were these copies?

I rifled through the desk drawers, finding only stationery, bills, and a half-finished letter to the village historical society about improper citation practices. No copies of mysterious journals, no treasure maps, nothing that looked remotely like "insurance" against shocking revelations.

Moving to the dressing table, I methodically searched each drawer. In the bottom one, beneath neatly folded scarves, I found a leather-bound book different from the journals. Smaller, older, with brass corner protectors and a faded wax seal on the cover.

My heart pounded as I carefully opened it. Instead of handwritten entries, I found newspaper clippings, photocopied documents, and handwritten notes—a research file of sorts. The first page bore the heading "Maria Constance —The Truth?" in my great-aunt's handwriting.

I began reading, quickly realizing this was no treasure hunter's notebook. It was a carefully documented investigation into the shipwreck's true cargo and purpose. According to my great-aunt's notes, the Maria Constance hadn't been carrying gold and antiquities as legend claimed, but something far more scandalous to Victorian society: documentation proving that several prominent local families were not who they claimed to be.

The Harbormaster's Journal apparently contained coordinates, not to sunken treasure, but to a hidden cove where the ship had been deliberately scuttled after unloading its cargo of forged documents, fraudulent lineage papers, and evidence of bigamous marriages that would have destroyed reputations and inheritances throughout Devon society.

Most damning was a list of family names involved in the conspiracy—wealthy merchants and minor nobility who had paid substantial sums to "improve" their family histories. At the top: Ashford.

I stared at the page, pieces clicking into place. According

to the research, the Ashford family's claim to their shipping fortune and social standing was built on fabricated documents that gave them rights to property, titles, and business partnerships they had no legitimate claim to. The Maria Constance had been carrying the original documentation that proved these frauds, along with evidence of illegitimate heirs who had been paid to disappear so that invented "proper" family lines could inherit instead.

The ship had been deliberately sunk in 1843 when authorities began investigating irregularities in various family claims. But the Harbormaster had kept records of exactly where the evidence had been dumped, creating a permanent threat to all the families involved.

If Victoria Ashford knew about these allegations and feared exposure, it would threaten not just her family's reputation but potentially their legal right to properties and wealth accumulated over generations. Court challenges from legitimate heirs could destroy the family financially.

A noise from downstairs jolted me back to reality—the distinctive sound of the back door opening. I froze, heart hammering. Had I locked it after Elliot left?

Hardy gave a low growl, while Austen's ears flattened against her head.

"Hello?" I called, trying to keep my voice steady. "Is someone there?"

Silence. Then footsteps on the stairs, too heavy to ignore or explain away.

I looked around frantically for a weapon, grabbing a heavy crystal paperweight from the desk. The dogs positioned themselves in front of me, Austen's usual primness replaced by a surprisingly intimidating stance.

The footsteps reached the top of the stairs. The bedroom door, already ajar, slowly pushed open.

"Ms. Hampton?" A uniformed police officer stepped into view, looking as startled to see me as I was to see him. "Oh! There you are. Sorry if I frightened you. The back door was open, and when you didn't answer my knock..."

I lowered the paperweight, exhaling shakily. "You could have called out."

"I did, ma'am." He eyed the dogs warily. "Multiple times."

I'd been so absorbed in my discovery that I hadn't heard him.

"How can I help you, Officer...?"

"Wells, ma'am. Detective Inspector Drake sent me to bring you back to the station. She has more questions."

The research file felt heavy in my hands. Should I bring it? Tell the police what I'd found? But if Victoria Ashford was involved in Thornbury's death and had connections to the force...

"May I ask what kind of questions?" I stalled, surreptitiously slipping the file beneath the journals.

"I couldn't say, ma'am. Just that it's urgent." He glanced at his watch. "DI Drake is waiting."

"Of course. Just let me get my coat and the dogs' leashes."

As the officer stepped back to allow me to pass, I made a split-second decision. I couldn't risk the file being discovered or confiscated before I understood its full implications. I needed to hide it somewhere safe, somewhere not obvious.

"Actually, I need to use the restroom first," I said. "Would you mind waiting downstairs? I'll just be a minute."

Once he was gone, I quickly removed the research file from beneath the journals and looked around the room. Where would be safe? Not here, where a thorough search would easily find it.

My eyes fell on a small decorative box on the dressing table—the kind that holds jewelry or keepsakes. I opened it to find a collection of vintage brooches. Lifting the velvet liner, I slipped the thin file underneath, then replaced everything exactly as I'd found it.

Not perfect, but better than carrying incriminating evidence to a police interview.

As I headed downstairs, my mind raced. What did DI Drake want? Had she found something in the shop? Did she know about the journal's true significance?

And most urgently—if the Harbormaster's Journal contained no treasure map but instead documented historical crimes that could ruin prominent families like the Ashfords, how far might someone go to keep that information buried?

Given Thornbury's fate, I feared I already knew the answer.

10

The police station seemed even more dismal the second time around. Constable Wells escorted me into the same interview room with its unforgiving lighting and uncomfortable chairs. Hardy and Austen were grudgingly allowed to accompany me after I pointed out that I had nowhere to leave them on short notice.

Hardy promptly sprawled across my feet while Austen sat at attention, eyeing the room's corners with suspicious dignity. Neither seemed impressed by law enforcement protocol.

I waited a full fifteen minutes before DI Drake appeared, carrying a clear evidence bag that made my stomach tighten. Inside was a leather-bound book with tarnished brass corners—a dead ringer for the description Freya had given of the mysterious document case my great-aunt had shown Thornbury.

"Miss Hampton," Drake greeted me, setting the bag on the table between us. "Thank you for coming in."

As if I'd had a choice. "How can I help, Detective Inspector?"

"We found this during our search of the bookshop's rare book room." She tapped the evidence bag. "Do you recognize it?"

I studied the book carefully. It looked old, its leather cover cracked and worn in places, with a distinctive wax seal visible even through the plastic. "I'm afraid not. As I mentioned, I've only been managing the shop for a few days."

"According to your employee, Malcolm Blackwood, this is the Harbormaster's Journal that Dr. Thornbury was so interested in seeing." She watched my reaction closely. "It was hidden behind a false panel in the display cabinet, not with the other manuscripts. Or should I say normally hidden there. Whatever happened in your rare books room, someone broke the panel and found the journal."

My pulse quickened. "Was it... tampered with? Is that why Thornbury was killed?"

"Interestingly, no. The journal appears untouched, which raises the question—if the killer found what they were looking for, why leave it behind?"

"Maybe they were interrupted," I suggested. "Or maybe they didn't recognize its significance."

"Perhaps." Drake opened a folder. "We've had a preliminary examination done by an expert from the county archives. His assessment is that this is indeed the logbook of Harbor Master Thomas Whitlock, dated 1843-1844."

"Starting the year the Maria Constance sank," I murmured.

Drake's eyebrow rose slightly. "You've done some research since our last conversation."

"I've heard village gossip," I corrected. "It's apparently quite the local legend."

"Indeed. The journal contains several entries referencing

the Maria Constance, including one dated the day of its sinking." She pulled out a photocopy of a handwritten page. "The interesting part is this entry, dated three days before the shipwreck."

She pushed the paper toward me. I read the elegant, faded script:

September 12, 1843 - Received instruction from H.A. regarding special arrangements for Maria Constance arrival. Northern cove to be cleared of all traffic. No official inspection to be recorded. Twenty pounds paid for discretion. God forgive me.

"H.A.?" I asked, though I had a sinking feeling I already knew.

"Henry Ashford, according to our historian. Ancestor of Victoria Ashford, who you met this morning."

I kept my expression neutral, not wanting to reveal that I knew more than I should. "I see. And you're telling me this because...?"

"Because when we searched Dr. Thornbury's home office, we found extensive research about the Ashford family's shipping interests. And a draft manuscript titled 'The Ashford Legacy: Falsified Papers and Hidden Lineages.'"

So Thornbury had discovered the same secret my great-aunt had documented.

"You think someone killed Thornbury to prevent publication of this research?" I asked carefully.

"It's a theory we're exploring." Drake studied me. "Your great-aunt granted Thornbury access to this journal after years of refusing. Do you know why she changed her mind?"

I thought of the journal entries I'd found. *The truth changes everything about the shipwreck, and the families deserve to know, whatever the consequences for old reputations.*

"No," I lied. "We weren't in regular contact about shop business."

Drake's expression suggested she didn't entirely believe me. "The timing is interesting. She grants access, then dies of supposedly natural causes. Thornbury continues his research, then is murdered in the same rare book room. And at the center of it all, a journal that implicates a prominent local family in smuggling falsified lineage papers long after such practices were banned."

She let the implication hang in the air between us.

"Are you suggesting my great-aunt's death wasn't natural?" I asked, my mouth suddenly dry.

"I'm not suggesting anything. I'm merely noting patterns." Drake closed her folder. "Did your great-aunt ever mention Victoria Ashford to you?"

"No. According to the village gossips, Ms. Ashford only moved here six months ago, not long before my great-aunt passed."

"That's correct. Though the Ashford family has historical connections to the area dating back centuries."

I remembered the research file hidden in my great-aunt's jewelry box. Should I mention it? But what if Victoria Ashford did have connections to the police? What if—

"Miss Hampton?" Drake interrupted my racing thoughts. "Is there something you'd like to share?"

"No," I said, perhaps too quickly. "I'm just trying to process all this. It sounds like something from a historical thriller, not real life."

"Murder is always real life to someone, Miss Hampton." Drake's tone was gentle but firm. "Dr. Thornbury's research put him on a collision course with powerful interests. We need to determine if those interests included someone willing to kill to protect a family name."

"And you think Victoria Ashford might be that someone," I stated rather than asked.

"I think anyone with motive, means, and opportunity deserves scrutiny. Ms. Ashford has been cooperative so far, providing alibis and documentation of her relationship with Dr. Thornbury."

This surprised me. "Alibis? For the night of the murder?"

"She claims to have been in London at a heritage preservation dinner. We're verifying with attendees and hotel staff."

So Victoria had a potential alibi. That complicated things.

"What about Malcolm?" I asked. "Has he explained why he was seen near the bookshop early that morning?"

Drake's expression sharpened. "Who told you that?"

"Village gossip again," I said smoothly. "Dr. Penrose apparently mentioned seeing him."

"Mr. Blackwood claims he was checking the shop's exterior as part of his morning routine, concerned about recent security issues. He states he noticed the door was secure and continued his walk."

"And you believe him?"

"We're verifying everyone's statements, Miss Hampton. Including yours." She leaned forward slightly. "Is there a reason you're particularly interested in Mr. Blackwood's whereabouts?"

I backpedaled quickly. "Not at all. I barely know him. I'm just trying to understand what happened."

"I'd advise focusing on reopening your business once we release the scene, rather than amateur detective work." Drake's tone remained professional, but the warning was clear. "History can be dangerous territory, particularly when it involves family reputations."

She stood, signaling the end of the interview. "You're free

to go, Miss Hampton. We'll be in touch if we have further questions."

"When can I reopen the shop?" I asked, gathering the dogs' leashes.

"We should be finished processing the scene by tomorrow afternoon. You'll be notified." She paused at the door. "One last thing—we found a stray cat in the upstairs storage room during our search. Animal control has been called."

My brain took a moment to process this. The gray tabby Elliot had mentioned—the stray my great-aunt used to feed. "Wait," I said. "That's... that's the bookshop cat. He belongs there."

It was a lie, but the thought of the poor creature being hauled off to some shelter seemed wrong.

Drake raised an eyebrow. "I was under the impression you weren't aware there was a cat."

"I meant he's a regular visitor," I amended. "A community cat, according to the locals. My great-aunt used to feed him. I'd like to continue the tradition."

After a moment's consideration, Drake nodded. "I'll have the officer inform animal control to leave him be. Assuming he's not evidence, of course."

"I don't imagine cats make very cooperative witnesses," I quipped, then immediately regretted trying humor in a murder investigation.

To my surprise, Drake's lips twitched slightly. "In my experience, they're worse than most human witnesses. Self-serving and prone to napping through critical moments."

With that unexpected glimpse of personality, she escorted me to the reception area where I found Freya pacing anxiously, several new pencils sprouting from her messy bun.

11

"Ginny!" Freya exclaimed, rushing over. "Are you all right? Are you being arrested? Do you need a lawyer? My uncle's a solicitor in Exeter—he mostly does wills and divorces, but he watches a lot of crime shows!"

"I'm fine, Freya," I assured her, touched by her concern. "Just helping with inquiries."

"That's what they say on TV when they think you did it," she whispered with wide eyes.

"I didn't do it." I guided her toward the exit, the dogs trotting alongside us. "But it seems someone might have killed Thornbury over historical research rather than rare books."

Outside, the late afternoon sun hung low in the sky, casting long shadows across the station car park. Freya linked her arm through mine as we walked.

"I called Dr. Harrington when I couldn't find you," she admitted. "He mentioned you were together earlier, and then when you weren't at the cottage, I panicked a bit."

"You called Elliot?" I wasn't sure whether to be embarrassed or grateful.

"Well, I didn't know who else to try! Malcolm wasn't answering his phone, and you don't really know anyone else yet." Her expression turned sly. "Dr. Harrington seemed quite concerned. Said he'd check the veterinary clinic in case you'd brought the dogs by."

"That was... thoughtful of him." I changed the subject quickly. "The police think they'll release the shop tomorrow afternoon. Would you be available to help with cleanup?"

"Absolutely!" Freya's enthusiasm returned full force. "I can come whenever you need. Oh! And I had an idea about how I could work while the shop is closed—virtual story hours! I mean, it's all about creating content for now. I thought I could read children's books on video and post them to social media. Get some community engagement going."

"That's actually brilliant," I said, genuinely impressed. "How long will it take you to set that up? Maybe its something we can just let run whether we're open or not."

"Already drafted a schedule and book list." She patted her oversized bag. "I was thinking three age groups: preschool, primary, and middle years. Plus maybe a special session featuring local Devon folklore?"

Her eagerness was infectious. Despite everything, I found myself smiling. "Draft a proper proposal and we'll discuss it over breakfast tomorrow."

"Brilliant!" She beamed, then sobered. "So what did the police want? If you can tell me, that is."

I hesitated, then decided a partial truth was better than outright lies. "They found the journal Thornbury was interested in. It contains historical information that could damage certain reputations. They think that might be why he was killed."

"Historical information? You mean like the treasure map?"

"Not exactly. More like evidence of historical wrongdoing by prominent families."

Freya's eyes widened. "Ooh, scandalous! Whose families?"

"I probably shouldn't say," I hedged. "It's an active investigation."

"Fair enough." She adjusted her bag. "Where are you headed now? Back to the cottage?"

I nodded, my mind on the research file hidden in my great-aunt's jewelry box. I needed to study it more thoroughly, figure out exactly what she'd discovered and why it had been worth killing for.

"Want company?" Freya offered. "I make a decent pasta if you're hungry."

The offer was tempting—I hadn't eaten since Elspeth's scones—but I needed time alone to process everything I'd learned.

"Rain check?" I suggested. "I'm exhausted and probably terrible company right now."

"Of course! Text if you need anything." She gave me a quick, unexpected hug before heading toward the bus stop.

I watched her go, feeling a mixture of gratitude and guilt. She was becoming a friend, yet I was keeping vital information from her. But the fewer people who knew about my great-aunt's research, the safer they'd be.

The walk back to the cottage took longer than usual, partly because the dogs insisted on investigating every hedge and lamppost, and partly because I took a circuitous route to avoid the village green where curious onlookers might still be gathered.

As I rounded the final bend to Cottage Lane, a familiar

figure stood from the bench beside my garden gate. Elliot straightened, hands in his pockets, looking oddly formal in the golden evening light.

"You're all right, then," he said by way of greeting.

"Were you waiting for me?" I asked, unable to keep the surprise from my voice.

"Freya called, concerned." He looked somewhat uncomfortable, as if being caught in an act of kindness was embarrassing. "I was on my way home. Thought I'd check."

It was a plausible explanation, except for one detail. "Your clinic is in the opposite direction."

"Yes, well." He cleared his throat. "Professional curiosity. Wanted to be sure the dogs weren't traumatized by two police visits in one day."

"The dogs are fine," I said, watching his face. "I'm fine too, thanks for asking."

"Good." He nodded awkwardly, then turned to leave.

"Do you want to come in?" I found myself saying. "I could use a sounding board again. And I have wine this time."

He hesitated, then nodded. "For a few minutes. I do have evening patients."

Inside, I uncorked a bottle of cabernet while Elliot filled water bowls for the exhausted dogs. We moved to the living room, where the evening sun streamed through the windows, illuminating dust motes that danced in the still air.

"The police found the journal," I said without preamble, taking a fortifying sip of wine. "The one Thornbury was after."

Elliot settled into an armchair, wine glass balanced on the arm. "And?"

"And it's not about treasure. It documents illegal smuggling of falsified lineage papers decades after such practices were banned. Specifically, by the Ashford family."

To his credit, Elliot didn't look shocked or skeptical. He simply nodded thoughtfully. "That would certainly be worth killing to conceal."

"Victoria Ashford claims she was in London the night of the murder. At some heritage preservation dinner."

"Convenient." He took a measured sip of wine. "Though not impossible to verify."

"The thing is..." I hesitated, then decided to trust him. "I found something in my great-aunt's bedroom. A research file she compiled about the Maria Constance. It contains newspaper clippings, photocopied documents, notes—all supporting the theory that the ship was involved in smuggling falsified documents about family lineages, with the Ashford family's full knowledge and profit."

Elliot's expression grew serious. "Where is this file now?"

"Hidden. I didn't want to hand it over until I understood exactly what I was dealing with."

"Withholding evidence from a murder investigation is a crime, Ginny."

"I'm not withholding evidence," I protested. "I'm... processing information."

He gave me a skeptical look.

"Fine. I'll give it to DI Drake tomorrow. But first I want to go through it properly, make copies." I set my glass down. "My great-aunt was trying to tell me something before she died. She wrote about making 'necessary arrangements' and securing the journal until I arrived. She made copies of key pages as 'insurance.'"

"Insurance against what?"

"I don't know." I rubbed my temples, feeling the beginnings of a headache. "But the last entry in her journal mentioned that 'the truth changes everything about the shipwreck, and the families deserve to know, whatever the consequences for old reputations.'"

"Families plural," Elliot noted. "Not just the Ashfords, then."

"Apparently not. But I haven't had time to review everything in the file."

Elliot was silent for a moment, swirling the wine in his glass. "Your great-aunt was a meticulous researcher. If she documented connections between prominent families and falsified lineage papers, it would cause more than embarrassment. There could be financial implications—inheritance disputes, property claims, loss of titles."

"Enough to kill for?"

"People have killed for far less." He set his glass down decisively. "You need to turn that file over to the police, Ginny. Tonight, not tomorrow."

"But what if—"

"If Victoria Ashford has influence with the police, DI Drake doesn't seem the type to be swayed by it. From what you've said, she's already investigating the historical angle."

He was right, of course. I was being paranoid and potentially obstructing justice.

"All right," I conceded. "I'll call Drake after you leave."

"I'll drive you to the station," he countered. "No more delays."

His firmness should have annoyed me, but there was something reassuring about it—a grounding presence amid the swirling theories and suspicions.

"Fine." I stood. "Let me get the file."

I headed upstairs to my great-aunt's bedroom, retrieving

the research file from beneath the jewelry box liner. As I turned to leave, a flash of gray outside the window caught my eye. I stepped closer, peering out at the garden below.

A figure moved stealthily along the hedge line—too tall to be Dot, too slight to be Dr. Penrose. As they passed beneath the porch light, I caught a glimpse of blond hair pulled into a chignon.

Victoria Ashford was prowling around my cottage.

I rushed back downstairs, file clutched to my chest. "Elliot," I hissed, finding him examining the bookshelves in the living room. "Victoria Ashford is outside."

He moved to the window with surprising speed, carefully peering through a gap in the curtains. "Where?"

"By the hedge—I saw her from upstairs."

He scanned the garden, then shook his head. "I don't see anyone now."

"She was there. Sneaking around like she was looking for something."

"Or someone," he said grimly. "We should call the police."

"And say what? I saw a woman walking past my garden? We need more than that."

Austen suddenly raised her head from her nap, ears perked. A moment later, Hardy joined her, both corgis staring intently at the back door. A faint scratching sound followed, then silence.

Elliot motioned for me to stay put, moving silently toward the kitchen. I ignored him, following close behind, file still clutched to my chest. The scratching came again—too high to be an animal, too deliberate to be the wind.

Someone was trying to get in.

Elliot reached for his phone, but before he could dial, a

crash from the front of the cottage made us both jump. The dogs raced toward the sound, barking furiously.

"Stay here," Elliot ordered, heading after them.

Again, I ignored him, because apparently I'd developed a death wish. We reached the front hallway together to find the window beside the door shattered, glass fragments scattered across the floor. The dogs stood barking at the broken window, but whatever—or whoever—had caused the damage was gone.

"Call the police," Elliot said, already dialing himself. "Someone's trying to get in."

I let him do the reporting while I checked on Austen and Hardy. No glass in their paws. I put the throw from the couch down for them to walk on, and ordered them to the kitchen where it was safe.

As emergency services responded with remarkable speed—the advantages of a small village—I clutched the research file and surveyed the damage. The break-in attempt seemed amateur and desperate. If Victoria Ashford was behind it, she was either very confident or very frightened.

Either way, I now had proof that my great-aunt's research was indeed worth breaking and entering for. The historical secrets of Tidehaven Cove were darker and more dangerous than I'd imagined when I inherited a quaint Devon bookshop. And someone was willing to go to increasingly extreme lengths to keep those secrets buried.

Standing amid broken glass with Elliot speaking to the police and the dogs maintaining their protective vigil from the kitchen door, I made a decision. I would not be intimidated out of my inheritance or my investigation. Someone had killed in my bookshop, threatened my home, and possibly hastened my great-aunt's death. They had made this personal.

And Virginia "Ginny" Hampton did not back down from personal challenges—especially not when they involved books, history, and justice long overdue.

12

"**A**bsolutely not," Constable Peters said when I suggested Victoria Ashford might be responsible for the break-in attempt. "Mrs. Ashford is at the Crown Inn having dinner with members of the historical society. At least a dozen witnesses can verify her whereabouts for the past two hours."

I deflated, perching on the arm of the sofa while forensic officers dusted the broken window frame for fingerprints. "Are you sure? I clearly saw someone with blond hair outside."

"Half the village is blond, Miss Hampton," Peters replied, not unkindly. "Including Sarah Mercer, who delivers evening papers and often walks through gardens as a shortcut."

"What about the break-in? That wasn't someone taking a shortcut."

"Could be local teenagers," Peters suggested. "We've had a few incidents of vandalism since the youth center closed. Or perhaps someone desperate enough to risk burglary. The murder has everyone on edge—perfect opportunity for opportunistic crime."

It was a reasonable explanation, yet it felt wrong. The timing was too convenient, especially after I'd discovered the research file.

Speaking of which, the file now sat in an evidence bag, duly logged and destined for DI Drake's desk in the morning. I'd summarized its contents for Constable Peters, who had taken notes with appropriate seriousness but seemed skeptical that historical research warranted breaking windows.

Elliot remained after the initial police response, making tea in my kitchen with the familiarity of someone who knew his way around. The dogs had settled near him, apparently having decided he was the most reliable human present.

"All finished, miss," announced one of the forensic officers. "We've boarded the window temporarily. You'll want proper repairs tomorrow."

"Thank you," I said automatically, trying to focus on practical matters rather than the unsettling feeling of my home being violated.

The officers departed with promises of increased patrols, leaving me alone with Elliot and two exhausted corgis in a cottage that suddenly felt much less secure.

"You don't believe the random vandalism theory either," I said as Elliot handed me a mug of tea.

"I think it's a remarkable coincidence that someone tried to break in hours after you discovered potentially incriminating historical documentation." He settled into the armchair opposite me. "Though Victoria Ashford having a public alibi complicates matters."

"She could have hired someone."

"Possible. Though rushing to hire a burglar on short

notice seems risky." He tapped his fingers thoughtfully against his mug. "Is there anyone else who knew you found the file?"

I thought back. "No one. I only discovered it this afternoon, then told you."

"And no one saw you hide it or retrieve it?"

"Just that police officer who came to fetch me, but I'd already hidden it by then." A troubling thought struck me. "Unless my cottage is being watched. The bedroom window overlooks the garden—someone could have seen me with the file."

Elliot frowned. "That's a disturbing possibility."

"This whole day has been disturbing." I sipped my tea, finding comfort in its warmth if not my circumstances. "Tomorrow I can finally reopen the shop, at least. Try to get back to something resembling normal life."

"With a murder investigation centered on your rare book room," Elliot pointed out. "Hardly normal."

"Bookshop by day, amateur detective by night. It's the classic cozy mystery setup." I attempted humor, but it fell flat even to my own ears.

Elliot didn't smile. "This isn't fiction, Ginny. Someone has already killed once. If they believe you have information that threatens them, you could be in genuine danger."

"Hence the broken window?"

"Perhaps a warning, or an aborted attempt to search for the file."

The matter-of-fact way he discussed potential threats should have been alarming, but I found his practicality reassuring. No histrionics, just clear-eyed assessment.

"What would you suggest? I can't exactly pack up and flee back to America."

"Why not?" he asked bluntly.

I blinked. "Because... because this is my home now. My great-aunt left me the bookshop and cottage for a reason. I'm not abandoning her legacy because someone's trying to scare me off."

My vehemence seemed to satisfy him. "In that case, we need to secure this cottage better, and you should not stay alone until the investigation concludes."

"We? Are you appointing yourself my security consultant, Dr. Harrington?"

"Someone needs to ensure you don't get yourself killed playing detective." The seriousness of his tone belied the almost teasing words. "Do you have anyone who could stay with you? Friends? Family?"

I shook my head. "I've been in Tidehaven Cove less than a week. The only people I know are my employees, my neighbors, and the local veterinarian who keeps showing up at crucial moments."

"Dot would likely volunteer," Elliot suggested. "She's surprisingly formidable despite appearances."

The thought of Dot Jenkins, armed with preserves and motherly concern, standing guard against murderous historical revisionists almost made me smile. Almost.

"Actually," I said slowly, "I was thinking of asking Freya. She mentioned she's having trouble with her roommate situation. Two birds, one stone."

"The enthusiastic assistant with the pencil collection in her hair?" Elliot seemed skeptical. "She's hardly intimidating."

"No, but she's observant, loyal, and has the energy of three normal humans. Plus, she's clever—studying for her master's in literature."

"It's your choice," he conceded. "Though I'd suggest additional security measures regardless. New locks, motion-sensing lights, perhaps a basic alarm system."

"My great-aunt managed fine with the original Victorian locks for decades."

"Your great-aunt wasn't investigating historical crimes linked to a recent murder," he countered.

Well, she was, but no one knew, so that was probably what saved her the trouble and vandalism. He had a point about security, annoyingly.

"Fine. I'll call a locksmith tomorrow." I set down my mug. "Thank you for staying through all this. Especially since you had evening patients."

"I rescheduled." He stood, collecting our empty mugs. "Mrs. Penrose's arthritic dachshund can wait another day for his checkup."

As he carried the mugs to the kitchen, I found myself studying him more carefully. Elliot Harrington was not what I'd initially assumed—not merely the reserved, slightly judgmental local vet, but someone with hidden depths and unexpected kindness. And he was handsome in an understated way, especially when that hint of a smile softened his features.

Stop it, I scolded myself. Finding the local vet attractive was straight out of a formulaic romance novel. Besides, I'd sworn off relationships after the Charlotte debacle.

Elliot returned, shrugging into his jacket. "I should go. Will you be all right tonight? That boarding on the window is temporary at best."

"I'll manage. The dogs are surprisingly good alert systems." As if on cue, Hardy raised his head and gave a single acknowledging woof before returning to his nap.

"Call if you need anything," Elliot said, heading for the door. "I live just beyond the mill—five minutes away."

"I will. And really, thank you again. For everything today."

He paused at the door, expression unreadable in the dim hallway light. "Be careful, Ginny. I've lived here all my life, and while Tidehaven Cove presents itself as a picture-perfect Devon village, it has hidden currents. Old families, old loyalties, old secrets."

"Now you sound like the cryptic local in a gothic novel," I teased gently.

That almost-smile appeared again. "Perhaps. But gothic novels often contain a grain of truth beneath the melodrama."

With that theatrical exit line, he was gone, leaving me alone in a cottage that suddenly felt too large and too quiet despite the dogs' presence.

13

Freya arrived as promised the next morning, bearing pastries from the bakery and enough enthusiasm to power a small city. She'd also brought a folder containing her virtual story hour proposal, complete with color-coded schedules and themed reading lists.

"This is impressive," I said, reviewing her meticulous plans over coffee at the kitchen table. "You've clearly put a lot of thought into this."

"I've wanted to do something like this for ages, but your great-aunt was a bit..." She hesitated.

"Traditional?" I suggested.

"Resistant to technology," Freya clarified diplomatically. "She thought reading should be a physical experience— paper, binding, the smell of books. Screens were, quote, 'the death of true literacy.'"

I smiled, hearing my great-aunt's crisp voice in the phrasing. "Well, I'm more pragmatic. If virtual story hours bring customers to the physical shop, I'm all for it."

"Exactly!" Freya beamed. "Oh, and I thought we could feature Captain in some of the videos! Kids love animals."

I glanced at the gray tabby, who was now sprawled across a sunny patch of kitchen floor with imperious confidence. Apparently not just the store cat. "Captain?"

"That's what everyone calls him. He's been wandering the village for years. Your great-aunt used to feed him, but she never let him inside because of her allergies." Freya tilted her head. "Looks like he's made himself at home, though."

"Temporary accommodation," I insisted, though I was already wondering where one purchased cat food in Tidehaven Cove. Or perhaps I could add it to my online order for Austen and Hardy.

A knock at the front door interrupted our planning session. Through the window, I spotted a police car parked at the curb.

"Ms. Hampton?" Officer Wells stood on the step, looking apologetic. "Detective Inspector Drake would like you to come to the bookshop. We're ready to release the scene, but she wanted you to check if anything's missing first."

"Of course." I grabbed my coat. "Freya, would you mind staying here with the dogs? And, apparently, the cat?"

"No problem!" She was already kneeling to greet Captain, who acknowledged her with a magnanimous head bump. "Take your time."

Officer Wells drove me to the village green, where a small crowd still lingered near the police tape surrounding Hampton's Books. I spotted Elspeth watching from her tea shop window, Dot chatting animatedly with several other older women, and Dr. Penrose standing slightly apart, observing with academic detachment.

DI Drake met me at the shop door, clipboard in hand. "Thank you for coming, Miss Hampton. We're finishing up now, but wanted you to verify the inventory before we release the scene completely."

"Has anything been taken?" I asked as she escorted me inside.

"That's what we need you to determine. Mr. Blackwood provided a partial inventory of the rare book collection, but said only you would have the complete picture."

That seemed unlikely, given Malcolm's three decades of employment versus my three days of ownership, but I didn't contradict her.

The shop looked unnervingly different—display units shifted, books disarranged during the search, fingerprint powder dusting various surfaces. It felt violated, like my cottage after the break-in attempt.

"Your employee did some preliminary cleaning yesterday," Drake explained, noting my expression. "But we had to re-examine several areas afterward."

Malcolm had been here? Without telling me? I filed away this information for later consideration.

"Where would you like me to start?" I asked.

"The rare book room, please. That's where we've identified the most significant disturbance, beyond the obvious crime scene."

I followed her up the creaking stairs to the top floor, trying to focus on the task rather than the mental image of Thornbury's body sprawled across the Oriental carpet. The rare book room had been thoroughly searched—glass-fronted cases stood open, manuscript boxes removed from shelves, display cases empty of their contents.

"Everything was photographed before being moved," Drake assured me. "And Mr. Blackwood supervised the handling of the rarest items."

Again, Malcolm's involvement without my knowledge. I

was beginning to feel like the titular owner but practical outsider in my own business.

"The Harbormaster's Journal was found here," Drake continued, indicating a display cabinet with a broken false back panel. "According to Mr. Blackwood, your great-aunt installed several such hidden compartments for the most valuable items."

"I wasn't aware," I admitted. "He hasn't shared those details with me yet."

Drake's expression revealed nothing. "Perhaps he was waiting for a more appropriate moment. Murder investigations tend to disrupt normal business transitions."

I couldn't argue with that logic. "What specifically do you need me to check?"

"Whether anything is missing compared to your understanding of the inventory. Particularly anything that might relate to the Harbormaster's Journal or the historical research Dr. Thornbury was conducting."

I scanned the room, aware of my limited knowledge but unwilling to appear completely incompetent. "I'll need to check against the inventory records. Where would those be kept?" The question was meant to prompt my own memories, but DI Drake supplied an answer.

"Mr. Blackwood mentioned a ledger in the main desk downstairs."

Of course he did. Another system he hadn't bothered to explain to me.

"I'll check that first, then," I said, heading back downstairs with Drake following.

The office behind the sales counter held a sturdy oak desk with numerous drawers. In the central drawer, I found a leather-bound ledger labeled "Special Collections" in Malcolm's precise handwriting. The detailed inventory included acquisition dates, condition notes, and valuation estimates for each item in the rare book collection.

"This seems comprehensive," I said, flipping through the meticulous entries. "It would take me some time to check everything against what's currently in the room."

"Perhaps focus on items specifically related to maritime history or the Ashford family?" Drake suggested.

I turned to the subject index at the back of the ledger, finding a section labeled "Devon Maritime History." Running my finger down the list, I noted several items related to shipping, harbors, and local vessels.

"There's an entry for 'Whitlock, T. - Harbormaster Records (1843-1844)' with an acquisition date of 1952," I said, turning to the referenced page. "That would be the journal you found, I assume."

"Correct. Anything else that seems related?"

I scanned the other entries. "'Merchant Shipping Logs - Devon Coast (1840-1850)' acquired in 1967. 'Ashford Brothers Shipping Company - Business Correspondence (1835-1860)' acquired in 1978." I looked up. "Those sound potentially relevant."

"Let's check if they're still in the collection."

We returned to the rare book room, where I located the merchant shipping logs in a manuscript box on the third shelf. The Ashford business correspondence, however, was nowhere to be found.

"According to the ledger, it should be in display case four, shelf two," I said, checking the empty space. "But I don't see it."

Drake made a note. "And you're certain it was part of the collection? Not sold or removed previously?"

"The ledger doesn't indicate any disposal," I replied, flipping through the detailed notes. "And it's marked as

'Not for Sale - Historical Significance' in Malcolm's hand-writing."

"Interesting." Drake's tone was neutral, but her attention had clearly sharpened. "Anything else missing?"

A thorough check against the ledger revealed two other absent items: a collection of newspaper clippings regarding the Maria Constance shipwreck, and a set of hand-drawn maps of the Devon coastline dated 1845.

"All items that might support or refute Thornbury's research about the Ashford family's connection to the documents on the ship," Drake observed. "That can't be coincidence."

"The killer took them," I concluded. "After killing Thornbury, they searched for and removed anything that might confirm his theories."

"But left the Harbormaster's Journal itself, which contained the most damning evidence," Drake mused. "Why take supporting documents but leave the primary source?"

"Maybe they didn't recognize its significance."

"Possibly." She made additional notes. "Or perhaps the killer was interrupted before completing their search."

By Malcolm? By me? The timing suddenly seemed crucial.

"When exactly did the murder occur?" I asked. "You mentioned between midnight and four AM, but can you narrow it down?"

"The medical examiner puts time of death around 2:30 AM, with a margin of error of an hour either way. Why?"

"Just trying to establish a timeline," I said casually. "If the killer was interrupted, knowing when might help identify by whom."

Drake gave me a measured look. "Leave the detective work to us, Miss Hampton. Your contribution is valuable, but identifying missing inventory is quite different from hunting a murderer."

"Of course," I agreed, though I had no intention of stopping my own investigation.

After confirming nothing else appeared missing, I signed the necessary forms allowing the police to release the scene. Drake assured me the shop could reopen tomorrow if I wished, though the rare book room would remain sealed with police tape for the time being.

"One more thing," Drake said as we descended to the main floor. "The research file you turned in last night—it contains some significant historical documentation. Would you mind telling me how your great-aunt acquired these materials?"

"I honestly don't know," I admitted. "I only discovered the file yesterday. From her journal entries, it seems she'd been researching the Maria Constance independently for some time."

"The file contains copies of documents that appear to be from the missing Ashford business correspondence," Drake noted. "Which suggests your great-aunt examined those materials thoroughly before they disappeared."

So the missing items weren't just valuable historical documents—they were potential evidence my great-aunt had already reviewed and partially copied. The implications made my skin prickle.

"Do you think my great-aunt's death might be connected to this?" I asked quietly.

Drake's expression remained professional. "We're reviewing all possibilities. The timing of her allowing Thornbury access to the Harbormaster's Journal, followed by her death and now his murder, creates a pattern that warrants investigation."

"You're reopening her case?"

"We're reviewing the medical reports and circumstances," she corrected. "Heart failure can have many causes, not all of them natural."

The possibility that had been lurking in my mind since finding my great-aunt's research was now an official police consideration. I wasn't sure whether to feel validated or terrified.

"I'd appreciate being kept informed," I said.

"Of course." Drake handed me a business card. "Call if you remember anything else about the missing documents. Or if you find any additional research materials your great-aunt might have secured elsewhere."

As she left, I remained in the silent bookshop, surveying the disarray. Reopening tomorrow seemed ambitious given the state of things, but the thought of admitting defeat, even temporarily, rankled. This was my shop now, my responsibility, my heritage.

14

The bell above the door jangled, pulling me from my thoughts. Malcolm stood in the doorway, his usual bow tie slightly askew, his expression uncharacteristically hesitant.

"Miss Hampton," he greeted me with a formal nod. "I see the police have finally departed."

"Malcolm." I didn't bother hiding my irritation. "Apparently you've been here already, helping with inventory."

"I was summoned yesterday to assist with identification of rare materials," he confirmed. "Detective Inspector Drake felt my expertise would expedite matters."

"And you didn't think to inform me?"

He straightened, defaulting to his most proper demeanor. "You were otherwise occupied with police interviews. I saw no reason to disturb you with matters I was perfectly capable of handling."

"Except they're not just your matters to handle anymore," I pointed out. "I'm the owner now, remember? Not just some temporary American placeholder until things return to normal."

A flicker of something—guilt? defensiveness?—crossed his face. "I've never suggested otherwise."

"You haven't needed to. Your actions make it perfectly clear." I took a steadying breath. "Malcolm, I appreciate your decades of service and your expertise. I really do. But we need to establish some boundaries and expectations. Starting with communication."

"Very well." His tone was stiff. "What would you like me to communicate?"

"For starters, why didn't you tell me about the hidden compartments in the rare book room? Or the detailed inventory ledger? Or the fact that items are missing from the collection—items specifically related to the research Thornbury and my great-aunt were conducting?"

Malcolm's expression shifted from defensive to alarmed. "Items are missing? Which ones?"

"The Ashford shipping correspondence. Newspaper clippings about the Maria Constance. Coastal maps from 1845." I watched his reaction carefully. "All things that might support theories about the Ashford family's involvement in falsified documentation."

He paled visibly. "This is... most concerning."

"Is it? Or is it exactly what you expected when you opposed my great-aunt granting Thornbury access to the Harbormaster's Journal?"

His head snapped up. "What do you know about that?"

"I found her journals," I said simply. "She wrote about your disagreement. About how 'the truth changes everything about the shipwreck, and the families deserve to know, whatever the consequences for old reputations.'"

Malcolm moved to the nearest chair and sank into it, suddenly looking every day of his age. "I never thought it would come to this. Murder. Break-ins. Police investigations."

"What exactly did you think would happen when historical evidence of historic lineage manipulation came to light?" I asked, pulling up a chair opposite him. "That everyone would politely agree to keep quiet for the sake of village harmony?"

"Your great-aunt believed in controlled disclosure," he said quietly. "Proper research, conclusive evidence, respectful presentation of facts. Not Thornbury's sensationalist approach."

"Yet she granted him access eventually."

"She did." His lips thinned in disapproval. "Against my strong objections."

"Why were you so opposed? Because you didn't want the Ashford family embarrassed?"

"Because I knew the backlash would be severe." He met my gaze directly. "Old families like the Ashfords don't simply accept historical revision that threatens their legacy and possibly their finances. They fight. Sometimes by legal means, sometimes... otherwise."

"Are you suggesting Victoria Ashford killed Thornbury to protect her family name?"

"I'm suggesting that powerful interests respond powerfully when threatened." He adjusted his bow tie nervously. "Your great-aunt understood this, which is why she proceeded cautiously. Thornbury had no such restraint."

"And what about you, Malcolm? Where do your loyalties lie?"

He looked offended. "With this shop. With its legacy. With your great-aunt's memory."

"Even if that means exposing uncomfortable truths about prominent local families?"

"Historical accuracy should prevail," he said stiffly. "But with appropriate sensitivity to communities affected. Thornbury cared only for sensation and personal glory."

I considered his words, trying to separate genuine principle from potential deflection. "Did you know the correspondence was missing when you helped with inventory yesterday?"

"No," he said firmly. "The police didn't allow a full accounting. They were primarily concerned with the Harbormaster's Journal itself."

"Which was found in a hidden compartment you never mentioned to me."

He had the grace to look abashed. "There are several such security features throughout the shop. Your great-aunt installed them over the years to protect the most valuable items. I was planning to review them with you once you'd... settled in."

"Once I'd proven I wasn't going to sell immediately, you mean."

"Once the day-to-day operations were running smoothly," he corrected diplomatically. "Recent events have rather disrupted the normal onboarding process."

I couldn't argue with that. Murder tends to rearrange priorities.

"I want to reopen tomorrow," I announced. "The main floor, at least. We can't access the rare book room anyway, and we need the income."

Malcolm looked around at the disarray. "That would require significant work tonight."

"Then we'd better get started." I stood, offering a small olive branch. "Unless you have other commitments?"

"Nothing that can't be rescheduled." He rose with

renewed energy. "I'll begin with the history section. It received the most disruption during the police search."

I sent a text to Freya telling her to stay at the cottage with the pets and continue working on her video ideas. I certainly didn't want Austen or Hardy sniffing around the store with all the mess. I assumed Captain would do as he pleased.

As Malcolm set to work with meticulous care, I started on the fiction shelves, grateful for the familiar, mindless task of alphabetizing and straightening. After an hour of silent industry, the shop began to resemble its former self. I was as relieved as Malcolm to see none of the books were sullied with fingerprint powder. Our efforts to remove it from other surfaces required more vigor than a book would survive.

"Malcolm," I said during a break, "what do you know about my great-aunt's relationship with the Ashford family?"

He paused, a stack of maritime histories balanced in his arms. "There was no relationship to speak of. The Ashfords left Tidehaven Cove generations ago, only returning when Victoria purchased the manor six months ago."

"But their history in the area goes back centuries?"

"Indeed. They were significant landowners and merchants in the nineteenth century, before the family fortune declined. The current Ashfords rebuilt their wealth in London, I believe, through property development."

"Like Victoria's company, Ashford Heritage Developments."

"Precisely." He shelved the books with practiced precision. "Though I understand the historical connection to Tidehaven Cove was a primary motivation for her purchase of the manor. Reclaiming family roots, as it were."

"Just in time to discover those roots might be tainted by historical criminal activity," I mused. "Convenient timing."

Malcolm gave me a sharp look. "Are you suggesting Mrs. Ashford knew about the journal before arriving?"

"It's possible, isn't it? If the family maintained connections to the area, they might have heard rumors about historical documents in the bookshop's collection. Even if their ancestors suppressed the truth."

"Thornbury wasn't exactly discreet about his research interests," Malcolm acknowledged. "He'd been inquiring about maritime records for years. It's conceivable word reached London."

"Prompting Victoria to return, assess the situation, and take steps to protect the family reputation," I concluded. "First by trying legitimate means—buying the manor, joining the historical society, establishing herself as a preservationist—then by more direct action when Thornbury got too close to the truth."

"A compelling theory," Malcolm admitted. "Though lacking concrete evidence."

"The missing documents might provide that evidence. If we could find them."

He shook his head. "If they were taken by the killer, they're likely destroyed by now."

"Unless they were taken for leverage. Historical documents proving families doctored their family trees would be valuable to certain parties—politicians, academics, activists."

"Blackmail, you mean?" Malcolm looked scandalized. "That seems rather sordid for a village bookshop dispute."

"Murder is already sordid," I pointed out. "Why not add blackmail to the mix?"

Our conversation was interrupted by the shop door opening. I turned, expecting Freya, but instead found Victoria Ashford herself standing in the entrance, looking polished and composed in a camel coat that probably cost more than my monthly rent in Charlotte.

"Miss Hampton," she greeted me with practiced warmth. "I heard the police had finally released your shop. I wanted to stop by and see how you were managing after such a dreadful ordeal."

Malcolm stiffened beside me, his posture radiating disapproval.

"We're doing our best to get back to normal," I replied neutrally. "Planning to reopen tomorrow."

"How ambitious." Her smile didn't reach her eyes. "Though I imagine customer confidence might be affected by recent events. Murder is so unsettling for potential browsers."

"Tidehaven Cove's residents are quite resilient," Malcolm interjected coldly. "The shop has stood for over a century. It will withstand this temporary unpleasantness."

Victoria turned her attention to him. "Mr. Blackwood, isn't it? Such dedication to remain after all these years. Your institutional knowledge must be irreplaceable."

The compliment sounded like a threat, somehow.

"My commitment is to the shop and its legacy," Malcolm replied. "Speaking of which, we have considerable work to complete before reopening. If you'll excuse us?"

Victoria's smile tightened. "Of course. I wouldn't dream of interrupting your preparations." She turned back to me. "Miss Hampton, if you reconsider your position about the property, my offer stands. Historical buildings require such specialized care, particularly after traumatic events. The financial burden can be overwhelming for new owners."

"I'm not selling," I said firmly. "But thank you for your concern."

"As you wish." She adjusted her designer handbag.

"Though I feel compelled to mention that buildings with violent histories often struggle to attract customers. There's something about bloodstains that dampens the browsing experience."

With that parting shot, she glided out, leaving a lingering scent of expensive perfume and thinly veiled threats.

"Well," I said into the silence that followed. "That wasn't remotely suspicious."

"Indeed." Malcolm's expression was grim. "It appears your theory about Mrs. Ashford may have merit. That was hardly a neighborly welfare check."

"More like a vulture checking if the carcass is ready for picking," I agreed. "She's getting desperate if she's being that obvious."

"Which makes her dangerous," Malcolm warned. "Desperate people take desperate actions."

I thought of my boarded window, the missing historical documents, and Thornbury's body on the Oriental carpet. "She's already taken desperate actions, Malcolm. The question is, what might she do next?"

As if in answer, my phone buzzed with a text from Freya: *Don't freak out but someone broke into your cottage again. I'm fine. Dogs fine. Cat missing. Police on way. Come home?*

I stared at the screen, my earlier bravado evaporating. This wasn't a cozy mystery novel anymore. It was a very real, increasingly dangerous situation where someone was willing to repeatedly break into my home to find... what? The research file was already with the police. What else could they be looking for?

Unless they didn't know I'd turned over the file. Unless they thought I still had evidence hidden somewhere.

Evidence worth killing for, worth breaking and entering for, worth terrorizing a newcomer for.

"Malcolm," I said, gripping my phone tightly, "did my great-aunt have a safety deposit box? Somewhere she might have stored important documents outside the shop?"

He frowned in concentration. "Not that she ever mentioned. Though she did maintain a small office at the cottage, separate from the main living areas. A converted garden shed, if I recall correctly. She used it for private research and correspondence."

A garden shed. The ramshackle structure I'd noted but not yet explored, assuming it contained nothing but gardening tools and cobwebs.

"I need to go," I said urgently. "There's been another break-in at the cottage."

"Good lord." Malcolm looked genuinely alarmed. "Were you expecting valuables from America?"

"No," I replied, heading for the door. "But I think someone else was."

I raced across the village green, my mind spinning with possibilities. If my great-aunt had used the garden shed as a private office, it might contain additional research materials —perhaps the "insurance" copies she'd mentioned in her journal. Copies the killer didn't know about, but suspected might exist.

Breaking points, I thought as I ran. We all have them— moments when safety, security, and certainty shatter. Mine had started with finding Thornbury's body, but now it was accelerating into something more personal, more threatening.

Someone was targeting my home, my historical inheritance, and possibly me. The quaint Devon bookshop fantasy had well and truly broken, revealing something darker and more dangerous beneath.

The question was whether I would break too, or find the strength to piece together not just a shop and a life, but the historical truth that had already cost at least one person's life—and might yet cost another.

15

I arrived at my cottage to find two police cars parked haphazardly outside and Freya pacing the front path, her hair even more chaotic than usual.

"Ginny!" She rushed toward me. "I'm so sorry! I just went to the bathroom for like three minutes, and when I came back, the kitchen door was wide open and Captain was gone and there were papers everywhere!"

"Are you okay?" I gripped her shoulders, scanning for injuries.

"I'm fine! Just freaked out. The dogs started barking like crazy, and when I went into the kitchen, whoever it was had already gone."

Constable Peters emerged from the cottage, notebook in hand. "Ah, Miss Hampton. Your assistant here has given us the basic details. Appears to be a quick in-and-out job. Kitchen door forced open, few drawers rifled through, nothing obvious taken according to Miss Collins."

"Captain's missing," Freya reminded him with surprising indignation. "The cat might have been taken."

Peters looked dubious. "More likely the animal bolted during the commotion. Cats are notoriously self-preserving."

I moved past them into the cottage. The kitchen showed signs of hasty searching—drawers left open, a chair over-turned, a scatter of mail across the floor. The newly installed back door lock had been forced, the frame splintered.

"They knew exactly when to strike," I observed. "After I left for the bookshop, but not immediately. I wonder if this perpetrator saw us cleaning up." But, how had they missed the fact that Freya was still inside if they were watching?

"Almost as if they were watching you," Peters agreed, suddenly more serious. "I've requested additional patrols for the area, and DI Drake is on her way."

I nodded absently, my focus already shifting to the garden beyond the broken door. Through the window, I could see the weathered garden shed at the back of the property. If Malcolm was right about my great-aunt using it as a private office...

"Did they go into the garden shed?" I asked sharply.

Peters consulted his notes. "Miss Collins didn't mention it. We've focused on the house so far."

"I need to check something." I headed for the back door.

"Miss Hampton, this is an active crime scene—"

I was already outside, striding across the lawn with Freya hurrying after me. The garden shed stood partially obscured by an overgrown lilac bush, its weathered boards and sagging roof making it look like a structure from a fairy tale rather than a home office.

The door was ajar.

"Is it supposed to be like that?" Freya whispered.

"I don't know. I haven't been inside yet." I approached

cautiously, noting fresh scrapes around the ancient padlock that now hung broken from the hasp.

"Should we wait for the police?" Freya asked, peering over my shoulder.

In answer, I pushed the door open.

The interior was nothing like the dilapidated garden shed I'd expected. Someone—my great-aunt, presumably—had transformed the space into a tidy study. Bookshelves lined one wall, a small desk occupied the center, and a reading chair sat beneath the single window. Everything was covered in a fine layer of dust—except for the desk drawers, which stood open and obviously recently searched.

"Whoa," Freya breathed. "Secret office much?"

I stepped inside, moving carefully to avoid disturbing potential evidence. The desk had been thoroughly ransacked, papers strewn across the floor. A faded photograph lay among them—my great-aunt standing beside a tall, distinguished man outside the bookshop, both smiling. I tucked it into my pocket without thinking.

"What were they looking for?" Freya wondered, staying respectfully by the door.

"The same thing they wanted at the cottage. The same thing Thornbury died for." I examined the bookshelves, noting gaps where volumes had been hastily removed. "Historical evidence."

Before I could investigate further, a sharp voice came from behind us. "Miss Hampton! Step away from that shed immediately!"

DI Drake stood in the garden, looking distinctly unimpressed with my amateur detective work.

"This is my property," I reminded her, though I did step outside.

"Which is now part of not one but two crime scenes," she

countered. "Contaminating evidence won't help us catch whoever's responsible."

She had a point, annoyingly.

"My great-aunt used this as a private office," I explained. "According to Malcolm, she did research here separate from the bookshop."

Drake's expression shifted from irritation to interest. "Research related to the Harbormaster's Journal and the Ashford family?"

"Possibly. The place has been searched, just like the cottage."

She signaled to a uniformed officer. "Secure this area and call the forensics team back." To me, she added, "Anything specific you noticed missing?"

"I wouldn't know. This is my first time seeing the inside."

Drake studied me for a moment. "Yet you immediately suspected it might contain something valuable—valuable enough for a second break-in on the same day. Why?"

I chose my words carefully. "After finding my great-aunt's research file, and learning about the missing documents from the shop, it made sense she might keep additional materials somewhere private."

"Logical." Drake nodded slightly. "Though that doesn't explain how our perpetrator knew about this particular location."

"They might not have, specifically," I suggested. "Maybe they were searching the cottage, saw the shed, and decided to check it too."

"Perhaps." She didn't sound convinced. "Though that would suggest our intruder had time to thoroughly search both locations before being interrupted—unlikely given Miss Collins' statement about the timing."

She was right. Whoever had broken in knew exactly

where to look and what they were after. Someone familiar with my great-aunt's habits. Someone from the village.

"I need to ask you and Miss Collins to remain available for additional questioning," Drake continued. "In the meantime, I strongly advise finding alternative accommodation until we're certain these break-ins have stopped."

"I'm not being driven from my home," I said firmly.

Drake's expression softened slightly. "It's not about retreat, Miss Hampton. It's about tactical positioning. You can't protect evidence or pursue truth if you're constantly defending your perimeter."

Put that way, it made practical sense rather than feeling like surrender.

"I could stay at the shop," I conceded. "There's a small apartment above it that my great-aunt used occasionally."

"Not the best since it was recently a crime scene. I'd suggest having someone stay with you."

"Already arranged. Freya's agreed to move in temporarily."

Drake nodded approvingly. "Intelligent precaution. Now, if you'll excuse me, I need to examine the shed before forensics arrives."

As she stepped inside, Freya tugged at my sleeve. "Um, Ginny? I think I just saw Captain."

I followed her pointing finger to the far corner of the garden where, indeed, a distinctive gray shape was slinking along the stone wall.

"He's okay!" Freya looked genuinely relieved. "I was worried someone took him."

"Cats are survivors," I said, watching as Captain paused to wash his face with deliberate unconcern, as if break-ins were beneath his notice. "Though I wonder where he was hiding."

"Should we try to catch him?"

"Let him come back on his own terms. He knows where to find us."

We returned to the cottage to find it swarming with police. Constable Peters was directing officers to take fingerprints from the kitchen door, while others photographed the disturbed contents of drawers and cabinets.

"Miss Hampton," Peters approached with an evidence bag. "We found this beneath the kitchen table. Does it look familiar?"

Inside was a small brass key with an ornate head.

"No," I said. "It's not mine."

"Might be the intruder's," he suggested. "Dropped during the hasty exit."

I studied it through the plastic. Something about it tickled my memory. "May I?"

He hesitated, then allowed me to examine the bag more closely. The key was old, its brass darkened with age except for the worn spots that suggested regular use. The head was shaped like a stylized ship's wheel.

"This looks like an antique," I said slowly. "Like something that might open an old box or cabinet."

"Or a hidden compartment in a bookshop," Peters suggested.

The connection clicked. "Like the ones in the rare book room? Where the Harbormaster's Journal was hidden?"

"Possibly. We'll need to check if it matches any locks at the shop."

Another piece of the puzzle, but what did it mean? Had the intruder been searching for a key to access something at the bookshop? Or had they dropped it accidentally while looking for something else?

"I should pack some things," I said, suddenly exhausted. "If I'm staying at the shop tonight."

"Of course." Peters stepped aside. "Officer Wells will accompany you upstairs. Just as a precaution."

I didn't argue. The cottage no longer felt like a sanctuary.

Upstairs, I threw together essentials while Officer Wells pretended not to watch from the doorway. Clothes, toiletries, my great-aunt's journal that I'd been reading—basic necessities for an indefinite displacement.

As I zipped my overnight bag, a movement outside the window caught my eye. A flash of gray, too large to be Captain, disappeared behind the garden shed. I moved closer to the glass, trying to see.

"Problem, miss?" Wells asked.

"Thought I saw someone in the garden." I craned my neck, but the angle was wrong. "Probably just a shadow."

But I knew it wasn't. Someone had been there—watching, waiting, assessing. Just as they'd been watching earlier, timing their break-in perfectly.

This was no opportunistic burglary. This was calculated, personal, and increasingly dangerous.

Twenty minutes later, Freya and I stood on the bookshop steps, bags at our feet, dogs on leashes, while Officer Wells unlocked the door. The shop felt different in the evening gloom—both comforting in its bookish familiarity and slightly ominous with its dark corners and creaking floorboards.

"The apartment access is through the back office," I told Freya, leading the way. "According to Malcolm, it's basic but functional."

"Basic is fine," she assured me. "I've been living with three other students in a flat the size of your kitchen.

Anything with less than four people fighting for the bath-room is luxury."

The narrow staircase behind the office door led to a small but surprisingly charming apartment. A sitting room with reading chairs and a kitchenette opened onto a bedroom with a double bed and a single tucked into an alcove. A tiny bathroom completed the space.

"This is perfect!" Freya enthused, immediately claiming the single bed. "Look, built-in bookshelves everywhere! Your great-aunt really embraced the whole bookshop aesthetic, didn't she?"

"She certainly had a theme going," I agreed, surveying the space that would be our sanctuary for the foreseeable future.

The dogs explored their new territory, sniffing curiously at unfamiliar corners. I filled water bowls while Freya arranged her belongings with the ruthless efficiency of someone accustomed to minimal space.

"So," she said once we'd settled with mugs of tea in the sitting room. "Secret sheds, multiple break-ins, mysterious keys... this is getting properly dramatic."

"Too dramatic for my taste," I admitted. "I came here to run a bookshop, not star in a mystery novel."

"But you're handling it like a pro." She tucked her feet under her, suddenly serious. "Most people would have packed up and fled by now."

Was I handling it like a pro? Or was I being foolishly stubborn, risking my safety for a legacy I barely understood?

"I can't leave," I said finally. "Not just because it would feel like giving up, but because I need to understand what my great-aunt was trying to protect. Why this historical research was worth killing for."

"And worth dying for?" Freya asked quietly.

The question hung between us. Had my great-aunt's heart failure been entirely natural? Or had her research put her in someone's crosshairs—someone who was now targeting me?

"I don't know," I admitted. "But I intend to find out."

Below us, the shop creaked softly in the evening silence, as if in agreement.

16

Morning arrived with thin sunlight filtering through unfamiliar curtains. For a moment, I stared at the ceiling in confusion before remembering—we were in the bookshop apartment, refugees from my twice-violated cottage.

The sounds of movement in the kitchenette told me Freya was already awake. I found her preparing tea with the focused intensity of a lab scientist.

"Morning!" she chirped, far too cheerfully for the early hour. "I found some tea bags and biscuits in the cupboard. Hope they're not ancient. The expiration date says last month, so probably fine?"

"Probably," I agreed, gratefully accepting a steaming mug. "Did you sleep okay?"

"Like the dead." She flushed immediately. "Sorry. Poor choice of words, considering."

"It's fine." I sipped the tea, which was actually quite good. "What time is it?"

"Just past seven. I thought we could get an early start on the shop. If we're still reopening today?"

I considered the question. With everything that had happened, postponing the reopening would be entirely reasonable. But the thought of surrendering to fear, of letting Victoria Ashford's veiled threats about "buildings with violent histories" prove correct, ignited something stubborn in me.

"We're definitely reopening," I decided. "Murder, break-ins, and historical scandals aside, we have a business to run."

"Brilliant!" Freya beamed. "I made a sign for the door —'Grand Reopening: Special Discount for Brave Browsers.' Too morbid?"

"Maybe lose the 'brave' part. Let's not remind customers they're entering a murder scene."

"Fair point. I'll rework it after breakfast."

The dogs needed walking, so we ventured out into the quiet village. Morning mist clung to the green, softening edges and creating a scene worthy of a tourism brochure—if you ignored the police tape still visible around my cottage in the distance.

Malcolm was waiting when we returned, punctual as ever despite the unusual circumstances. He raised an eyebrow at my casual attire but mercifully withheld comment.

"I've brought fresh pastries," he announced, lifting a white bakery box. "Mrs. Thatcher at the bakery sends her regards and insisted these were 'on the house'—her words, not mine."

"That's very kind." I accepted the box, touched by the gesture. "We're having our grand reopening today."

"Indeed." His expression remained neutral. "The constable mentioned you'd be staying in the apartment for the time being. A prudent decision."

"Not really a decision so much as a necessity." I led the

way into the shop. "Someone is very determined to find whatever my great-aunt was researching."

Malcolm busied himself with the cash register. "The police have not shared any theories regarding suspects?"

"Nothing concrete. Victoria Ashford had an alibi for the first break-in, but the second occurred while I was at the shop talking to you."

"Convenient timing," he observed. "Almost as if the perpetrator knew you would be occupied."

The implication hung in the air between us.

"You think someone's watching my movements?" I asked, voicing what we were both thinking.

"It would explain the precision of the timing." He straightened a stack of bookmarks with unnecessary care. "Have you considered that someone in the village might be... informing on your activities?"

"You mean like a spy? That seems a bit dramatic for Tidehaven Cove."

"Murder is already quite dramatic for Tidehaven Cove," he pointed out. "And historical reputations have inspired worse betrayals than gossip."

Before I could pursue this unsettling line of thought, Freya bounded down from the apartment, now dressed in what appeared to be her professional best—a floral dress only slightly creased, hair somewhat tamed, and just three pencils visible in her bun.

"Ready for reopening!" she announced. "I updated the sign and put some books in the window that seemed appro-priate—though I wasn't sure about including 'And Then There Were None.' Too on the nose?"

"Perhaps a touch macabre," Malcolm agreed dryly. "Though I appreciate the literary connection."

The three of us worked steadily until opening time,

arranging displays, dusting shelves, and restoring the shop to its pre-police-search state. By nine o'clock, Hampton's Books looked welcoming and deliberately normal, as if murder were simply an inconvenient interruption in regular business.

Our first customer arrived precisely at opening—Dot, who made a great show of browsing before selecting a gardening book that I suspected she already owned.

"Such a relief to see the shop open again," she enthused at the register. "The whole village is talking about it. Most supportive, of course, though Oliver Blackthorn was telling anyone who'd listen at the pub last night that you'd be closing within the week."

"Was he?" I kept my tone light. "Well, he'll be disappointed."

"I told him as much! Said the Hamptons have run this shop through two world wars and the great flood of '68. Takes more than a bit of unpleasantness to shut it down." She leaned closer. "Though do be careful, dear. Some people don't like their secrets disturbed."

I wondered what secrets Dot might be referring to, but before I could ask, the door chimed again. Three more customers entered, then two more, creating a steady trickle that gradually became a respectable flow. By lunchtime, we'd made more sales than any day since my arrival.

"Nothing like murder to boost business," Freya whispered during a brief lull. "Everyone wants a look at the crime scene."

She wasn't wrong. While most customers made legitimate purchases, I caught more than a few casting furtive glances toward the police-taped staircase leading to the rare book room.

During the afternoon rush—apparently a genuine

phenomenon in Tidehaven Cove, where early closing hours meant concentrated shopping time—a familiar face appeared at the counter. Elliot stood examining a veterinary text, looking somewhat out of place among the browsing tourists.

"Busy day," he observed as I approached. "Your grand reopening seems successful."

"Morbid curiosity is good for business, apparently." I gestured to the book he held. "Finding anything interesting?"

"Actually, yes. This text on nineteenth-century animal husbandry has some unusual annotations." He opened to a marked page. "See here? These margin notes reference breeding methods specific to transportation conditions on long sea voyages."

I studied the faded handwriting. "You think it's related to the Maria Constance?"

"Possibly. Cargo ships often carried livestock alongside other goods. If this book belonged to someone involved with such vessels..." He left the implication hanging.

"I'll set it aside for further examination," I decided, taking the volume. "Though I'm guessing you didn't come in just to browse historical veterinary practices."

"No." His expression grew serious. "I wanted to check if you were all right after yesterday's events. I heard about the second break-in."

"News travels fast."

"Small village, big mouths," he said wryly. "Are you and the dogs settled at the apartment?"

"As settled as possible under the circumstances. Freya's staying with me too."

He nodded approvingly. "Good. Safety in numbers.

Though I'd suggest maintaining irregular patterns in your movements. If someone is watching you—"

"I know. Don't be predictable." I sighed. "I came here for a quiet life running a bookshop. I wasn't expecting to need counter-surveillance techniques."

That hint of a smile appeared briefly. "Life rarely matches our expectations. Sometimes that's for the better."

Was he flirting? Before I could decide, Freya appeared at my elbow.

"Sorry to interrupt, but Mrs. Ashford is here." She kept her voice low. "Looking very determined in the history section."

I glanced over to see Victoria Ashford examining a book with obvious pretense, her attention clearly on our conversation.

"Keep an eye on her," I murmured to Freya. "I'll be right there."

Turning back to Elliot, I found his expression had hardened as he too watched Victoria.

"Be careful," he said quietly. "If she has something to hide—"

"I know. Don't worry, I'm not planning to accuse her of murder on the shop floor." I tried for lightness, but his concern was touching. "Thanks for checking in."

He nodded once, then selected a different book. "I'll take this one. Consider it support for your reopening."

As he moved to the register where Malcolm presided, I steeled myself and approached Victoria, who abandoned all pretense of browsing as I neared.

"Miss Hampton," she greeted me with practiced warmth. "How brave of you to reopen so quickly after such disturbing events."

"Thank you for your concern," I replied neutrally. "Was there something specific you were looking for today?"

"Just browsing, really. Though I am interested in your local history section. I understand some of your rarer volumes are currently... inaccessible."

The pointed reference to the sealed rare book room was impossible to miss.

"The police are still processing evidence," I confirmed. "But our general collection remains available."

She replaced the book she'd been holding with deliberate care. "I was sorry to hear about the break-ins at your cottage. Such a violation of one's personal space. I do hope nothing irreplaceable was taken?"

Her emphasis on "irreplaceable" sent a chill down my spine. She knew about the garden shed. Somehow, she knew exactly what had been targeted.

"Just peace of mind," I replied lightly. "Though the police did find an interesting clue—an antique key that might match certain locks in the shop. They're very hopeful it will lead to the perpetrator."

I watched her face carefully, but if my improvised misdirection affected her, she didn't show it. Her composure remained impeccable.

"How fascinating," she murmured. "Though keys can be such common items, can't they? I have several antiques myself—family heirlooms with no known locks. Decorative, really."

"This one had a distinctive ship's wheel design," I pressed. "Quite unique."

For the briefest moment, something flickered in her eyes —recognition? concern?—before vanishing behind her polished facade.

"How nautical. Appropriate for a seaside county." She

glanced at her watch. "I should be going. Historical society meeting this evening—we're discussing preservation grants for the manor restoration."

"Of course. Wouldn't want to keep you from preserving history."

The double meaning wasn't lost on her. She smiled thinly. "Some history deserves preservation, Miss Hampton. Other aspects are better left in the past. Good day."

As she departed, I noticed Elliot watching the exchange from near the door, his expression troubled. Our eyes met briefly before he too left, the bell jangling in his wake.

The rest of the afternoon passed in a blur of customers, sales, and the comforting routine of bookselling. By closing time, the till was satisfyingly full and the shelves noticeably depleted.

"Successful day," Malcolm noted as he tallied the final receipts. "Perhaps our best in months."

"Nothing sells books like scandal," Freya quipped, collapsing dramatically into an armchair. "My feet are killing me."

I locked the door with relief, flipping the sign to "Closed" and drawing the blinds. The shop felt different in the evening quiet—both sanctuary and potential trap. Somewhere upstairs, beyond the police tape, lay the scene of Thornbury's murder. And somewhere in the village, his killer walked free.

As Malcolm prepared to leave, he hesitated by the door. "Miss Hampton, a word of advice, if I may?"

"Of course."

"Be cautious with that veterinarian. Dr. Harrington has lived here all his life. His connections to local families run deep."

I frowned. "You think Elliot is involved somehow?"

"I think in small villages, loyalties are complex and often invisible to outsiders." He adjusted his bow tie. "That's all. Good evening."

With that cryptic warning, he departed, leaving me to wonder if there was anyone in Tidehaven Cove I could truly trust.

17

"Any idea why Malcolm would warn you about Dr. Harrington?" Freya asked later as we shared take-away curry in the apartment. "They seemed perfectly civil to each other in the shop."

I pushed a piece of chicken toward Hardy, who was watching my plate with undisguised longing. We'd ordered some plain meat anticipating the dog's needs. "No idea. Just another village mystery to add to the collection."

"It's weird though, right? I mean, everyone respects Dr. Harrington. He saved Mrs. Potter's ancient retriever last year when everyone thought it was a goner."

"Saving dogs doesn't automatically make someone trust-worthy," I pointed out, though I privately agreed with her assessment. Elliot had given me no reason to distrust him—quite the opposite.

"True, but..." Freya hesitated. "Malcolm's been acting odd lately. Even before you arrived. Your great-aunt mentioned it in her last weeks."

This was new information. "What did she say exactly?"

"That Malcolm was becoming 'excessively protective' of

certain materials. That he'd 'forgotten his true duty was to knowledge, not reputation.'" Freya pushed her food around thoughtfully. "I thought it was just end-of-life philosophical stuff, you know? But now I wonder if it was about the Harbormaster's Journal."

The pieces were aligning differently. Malcolm's resistance to Thornbury's access. His failure to disclose the hidden compartments. His absence during crucial moments.

"Do you think Malcolm could be involved in Thornbury's death?" I asked quietly.

Freya's eyes widened. "Malcolm? But he's so... proper. I can't imagine him hurting anyone."

"People can surprise you." I thought of Victoria Ashford's perfectly manicured hands and wondered if they had wielded a brass bookend with deadly force. "Especially when protecting something they value."

"But what would Malcolm be protecting? He's devoted to the shop."

"Maybe it's not what, but who." I recalled his comment about village loyalties. "What if his warning about Elliot was actually misdirection? Pointing suspicion elsewhere?"

Freya didn't look convinced. "That's pretty devious for someone who leaves notes about proper holding of hardcover book spines."

She had a point. Malcolm's fussiness seemed at odds with calculating murderer. But still, something felt off about his behavior.

"Let's table the Malcolm mystery for now," I suggested. "We have more immediate concerns—like figuring out what was in that garden shed that someone wanted badly enough to break in twice."

"And what the ship's wheel key opens," Freya added,

warming to the investigation. "Something at the bookshop, presumably. Something hidden."

"Possibly something in the rare book room, which is conveniently sealed off by police tape."

"We could ask DI Drake for access," Freya suggested. "For inventory purposes."

"Worth a try." I gathered our empty containers. "But first, we should do what any good investigators would—research."

Freya's eyes lit up. "The shop's closed. We have thousands of books at our disposal. And I happen to know where your great-aunt kept the local history collections."

Twenty minutes later, we'd assembled a research station in the main shop, surrounded by stacks of books on Devon maritime history, local genealogy, and nineteenth-century shipping records. Austen curled disdainfully on a nearby chair while Hardy sprawled across my feet, both apparently unimpressed by our literary detective work.

"Here's something," Freya said eventually, looking up from a hefty tome. "The Ashford family shipping business began in 1820, founded by brothers Henry and William Ashford. They specialized in 'exotic goods from the colonies,' whatever that means."

"Probably sugar, tobacco, cotton," I suggested. "The usual colonial commodities."

"Right. They were super successful until 1845, when there was some kind of scandal that's only vaguely referenced. The business continued but never regained its former prominence." She frowned at the page. "That's oddly close to when the Maria Constance sank in 1843."

"Too close to be coincidence." I pulled another book from the stack. "Let's see if we can find more about that scandal."

We continued our literary excavation, piecing together fragments of history like an archaeological dig. The picture that emerged was troubling. The Ashford brothers had indeed built their fortune on colonial trade, primarily from the West Indies and Africa. The scandal that damaged their reputation involved allegations of smuggling, though details were frustratingly scarce in official records.

"It's like there's a deliberate gap in the historical narrative," I noted, comparing several accounts. "Everyone acknowledges something happened, but no one specifies what."

"Intentional obfuscation," Freya agreed. "Someone wanted this part of history buried."

"But my great-aunt found something in the Harbormaster's Journal that changed everything," I mused. "Something that 'the families deserve to know, whatever the consequences for old reputations.'"

A thought struck me. "Families, plural. Not just the Ashfords were implicated."

"Other local merchants?" Freya suggested. "Or maybe officials who looked the other way?"

The bell over the door jangled suddenly, making us both jump. I'd forgotten to lock up after Malcolm left.

Dr. Penrose stood in the entrance, looking surprised to find us surrounded by books on the floor. "Am I interrupting something?"

"We're closed, actually," I said, rising to my feet. "Just doing some after-hours research."

"Ah." He surveyed our literary chaos with academic interest. "Local maritime history, I see. Fascinating subject, particularly the less documented aspects."

Something in his tone made me pause. "Did you need something specific, Dr. Penrose?"

"Indeed." He closed the door behind him. "A private word, if possible. About Victoria Ashford and her sudden interest in historical preservation."

Freya and I exchanged glances. "What about her?" I asked cautiously.

"I believe she is not what she appears to be." He removed his glasses, polishing them methodically. "Nor are her motivations for purchasing Tidehaven Manor what she claims."

"And you're telling me this because...?"

"Because I too have been researching the Maria Constance incident." He gestured to our books. "With considerably more success, I might add. And because I believe your great-aunt was killed to prevent her sharing what she had discovered."

The blunt statement hung in the air between us.

"You think her heart failure wasn't natural," I said finally.

"I think certain toxins can induce symptoms nearly indistinguishable from natural cardiac events, particularly in older individuals with pre-existing conditions." His clinical tone made the accusation even more chilling. "Your great-aunt was in excellent health for her age. Her sudden decline was... notable."

"Why are you telling me this now?" I demanded. "Why not go to the police?"

"Accusations without evidence are merely slander," he replied. "I needed more proof. And I believe you may have found some—in your great-aunt's garden shed."

So he'd been watching too. "The police have secured the shed as a crime scene."

"Unfortunate, but not insurmountable." He reached into his pocket and withdrew a slim leather portfolio. "Perhaps this might help your investigation."

I accepted it cautiously. Inside were photocopies of what

appeared to be private correspondence—letters dated 1843, addressed to the Harbor Master from someone identified only as "H.A."

"Henry Ashford," Dr. Penrose confirmed, noting my recognition. "Instructing special arrangements for a chest to be delivered outside normal channels. No inspection, no documentation."

"Package? So information? Documents?," I murmured.

"Precisely." He looked grimly satisfied. "In that period, legitimacy was everything. The Victorians were avid collectors of lineage, provenance, any record that could prove value or connection."

"Where did you get these?" I asked.

"Your great-aunt shared them with me shortly before her death. We were collaborating on research about local maritime history—my academic specialty. She discovered these among the bookshop's archives and recognized their significance immediately."

"Why would she share them with you but not Malcolm?"

"Malcolm Blackwood is many things—efficient, knowledgeable, dedicated. But he is also deeply connected to old Tidehaven Cove families and their networks of obligation." Dr. Penrose reclaimed the portfolio. "Your great-aunt recognized that such revelations required a more... objective perspective."

"Like yours?" I couldn't keep the skepticism from my voice.

"I am an outsider here, despite my years of residence. Academia has taught me to value truth over comfort. Vivian appreciated that quality." He tucked the portfolio away. "As did Thornbury, despite his many flaws."

"You were working with Thornbury too?" Freya asked incredulously.

"Not collaborating, precisely. More... parallel investigations with occasional information exchange." He sniffed disapprovingly. "His methods were sensationalist, but his research was sound."

The pieces were reconfiguring again. "So when Thornbury gained access to the Harbormaster's Journal—"

"He found confirmation of what we had begun to suspect. That the Ashford family's fortune was built not merely hard work as they claimed. A secret in their past changed their fortunes at a critical time. Not only the Ashfords, but other families in the neighborhood."

"Something that would have power even after all this time," I concluded.

"Indeed. Though I suspect she already knew that history, or at least suspected it. Her acquisition of the manor and sudden interest in local heritage societies coincided too neatly with Thornbury's increasingly public research efforts."

"She came to contain the damage," I realized. "To find and destroy evidence before it became public."

"A reasonable assessment." Dr. Penrose checked his watch. "I should go. I've said more than is prudent already."

"Wait," I stopped him. "Why tell me all this? Why now?"

"Because unlike Victoria Ashford, I believe the truth deserves revelation, however uncomfortable. And because your continued investigation puts you in considerable danger." His expression softened slightly. "Vivian was my friend. I failed to protect her. I would not see her great-niece suffer the same fate."

With that unsettling farewell, he departed as abruptly as he'd arrived, leaving Freya and me staring at each other in stunned silence.

"Well," Freya said finally. "That was dramatically cryptic."

"But informative," I countered. "If he's telling the truth, we now have confirmation that my great-aunt was murdered and that Victoria Ashford may indeed be the killer."

"Or it could be misdirection." Freya looked troubled. "Like, what if Dr. Penrose is actually involved somehow? Maybe he's trying to point suspicion away from himself?"

"By revealing what he knows about the Ashfords?" I shook my head. "That doesn't make sense."

"Unless what he knows isn't actually damaging to himself but is to others." She began gathering the scattered books. "This is getting complicated."

She wasn't wrong. Every new piece of information seemed to reconfigure the puzzle rather than solve it. Victoria Ashford, Malcolm, Thornbury, my great-aunt, Dr. Penrose—the relationships and motives kept shifting like the pieces in a kaleidoscope.

"Let's call it a night," I suggested. "My brain is spinning, and we have actual work tomorrow."

As we tidied our research materials, my phone buzzed with a text. Unknown number: *Check your great-aunt's first edition of Treasure Island. Third shelf, fiction section. -A friend*

"What is it?" Freya asked, noting my expression.

I showed her the message. "Either helpful information or an elaborate trap."

"Only one way to find out." She headed for the fiction section, scanning the shelves. "Here it is! First edition—well, facsimile first edition. Should I get it?"

"Might as well," I sighed. "Though this cloak-and-dagger routine is getting old."

The book looked unremarkable from the outside—a nice but not exceptional copy of Stevenson's classic. Freya handed it to me with the reverence reserved for potential evidence.

I opened it carefully. At first glance, nothing seemed unusual—until I noticed a slight thickness to the back endpaper. Pressing gently, I felt something concealed beneath it.

"There's something here," I murmured, examining the binding more closely. "The endpaper's been modified."

Using a letter opener from the counter, I carefully separated the glued edge. A folded paper slid out—not centuries-old historical evidence, but a modern photocopy of what appeared to be a handwritten list of names with dates beside them.

"What is it?" Freya peered over my shoulder.

"I'm not sure." I unfolded it fully. "Looks like a list of people, maybe a dozen names. All with the same date—April 15, 2020."

"The day your great-aunt died," Freya whispered.

A chill ran down my spine as I registered the significance. This wasn't just historical evidence—this was something much more immediate. A list of people connected to my great-aunt's death, hidden for me to find.

The question was: who had hidden it? And why direct me to it now?

18

"I should take this to DI Drake immediately," I said, carefully refolding the mysterious list of names we'd found in the copy of Treasure Island.

Freya bit her lip. "Are you sure? We don't even know what it means yet. Maybe we should investigate a bit first?"

"Investigate how? I don't recognize any of these names except my great-aunt's."

"But that's exactly why we should look into it!" She tapped the paper excitedly. "If someone wanted the police to have this, they would have sent it to DI Drake directly. Instead, they texted you. That suggests they want you to find something before involving the authorities."

Her reasoning was surprisingly sound. "Or they're setting me up to withhold evidence."

"Possibly." She didn't look deterred. "But consider this—that text came from someone who knows the shop's inventory intimately. Someone who knew exactly where this book was shelved."

"Malcolm," I concluded. "Or possibly my great-aunt herself, if she set this up before she died."

"Either way, there's a reason they wanted you to find it first. We should at least try to understand what these names mean before handing it over."

I glanced at my watch. Nearly midnight. "Let's sleep on it. We can decide in the morning what to do."

But sleep proved elusive. I lay awake in the unfamiliar bed, the list of names tumbling through my mind like lottery numbers waiting to reveal their significance. Who were these people? What connected them to April 15, 2020 —the day my great-aunt died?

MORNING ARRIVED with no clarity but a firm decision. I would take the list to DI Drake, but first, I'd make a copy. Proper procedure versus pragmatic precaution.

I found Freya already awake, laptop open at the tiny kitchen table. "I've been researching," she announced without preamble. "Three of the names on that list are local historical society members. Two others are on the village council."

I blinked, impressed. "How did you figure that out so quickly?"

"Facebook stalking and the Tidehaven Cove community newsletter archive." She grinned. "Online research is literally what I do for my thesis. Anyway, all these people were at a historical society fundraiser the night before your great-aunt died."

"That can't be coincidence."

"Definitely not. And guess who else was there?" She spun her laptop to show me a digital photograph. "Victoria Ashford, newly arrived in the village and making her social debut."

The image showed a group of well-dressed people

raising champagne glasses in what appeared to be Tide-haven Manor's grand entrance hall. Victoria stood at the center, resplendent in navy blue, playing the gracious hostess.

"She held the fundraiser at the manor," Freya explained. "Her first public event after purchasing the property. According to the newsletter, it was 'a celebration of local heritage and the beginning of an ambitious restoration project.'"

"And the very next day, my great-aunt—who had discovered the Ashford family's historical crimes—conveniently died of heart failure." The implications were chilling. "We need to take this to Drake."

"Now we're talking." Freya closed her laptop. "But shouldn't we check out a few more angles first? Like maybe talk to someone who was at that fundraiser?"

"That would be interfering with a police investigation."

"Only if we mention the list," she countered. "We could just ask general questions about the event. People love talking about fancy parties they attended."

I was tempted by her reasoning, even as the rational part of my brain screamed about proper procedure and leaving detective work to professionals. But then, hadn't Drake herself said I had access to people and places the police didn't?

"One conversation," I conceded. "With someone unlikely to be involved in my great-aunt's death. Then we take everything to Drake."

"Deal!" Freya's enthusiasm was slightly alarming. "I vote we talk to Mrs. Thatcher from the bakery. She's on the list and provided catering for the fundraiser. Plus, she gives extra pastries to people she likes, which is definitely us after buying three of her specialty loaves yesterday."

"You've really thought this through."

"Amateur sleuthing is literally my dream job. After finishing my thesis, obviously."

An hour later, we stood in Mrs. Thatcher's fragrant bakery, having timed our arrival during the mid-morning lull. The plump, flour-dusted proprietor beamed at our purchase of cherry scones.

"Supporting local businesses after everything you've been through," she clucked approvingly. "Your great-aunt would be proud. She always said community was the heart of Tidehaven Cove."

"She spoke of you often," I improvised. "Mentioned you were both on the historical society committee?"

"Oh yes, for years! Vivian handled the archives while I organized the refreshments." She wrapped our scones with practiced efficiency. "Such a shame she missed our grandest event—that fundraiser at the manor last April. Taken ill that very morning, poor dear."

My pulse quickened. "The morning of the fundraiser? I thought she attended?"

"Oh no, dear. Called me at dawn with terrible chest pains, asking me to handle the society's presentation in her place. I went straight over," Mrs. Thatcher's voice broke and her eyes grew misty. "The doctor put her on a course of new pills. But by the next morning... Well, at least she didn't suffer long."

This contradicted everything we'd assumed. "So she was seriously ill the morning of the fundraiser, not the day after?" I supposed I'd assumed the illness and death came one after the other.

"The very morning. April 14th. We almost canceled, but Reverend Williams said Vivian would have wanted it to proceed. He was so confident the doctor's prescription would work"

"Who else was with her? When she died, I mean."

Mrs. Thatcher considered this while adding an extra scone to our bag. "Just me at first, then Dr. Campbell, though he was too late, poor man. The police came afterward, of course, as they do for any unattended death. And Malcolm arrived just as they were... taking her away." Her voice dropped. "Absolutely distraught, he was. Never seen him so undone."

"Malcolm was there?" This was new information.

"Arrived from the shop. Said Vivian had called him, but he'd been shelving new arrivals in the basement and missed it. Blamed himself terribly." She shook her head. "Though between us, I always thought it odd she called both of us so early. Almost as if she knew something was wrong before it happened."

Or as if she suspected something was about to happen. Had my great-aunt sensed danger? Called potential witnesses as a precaution?

"Thank you, Mrs. Thatcher." I accepted our overstuffed bag. "You've been very helpful."

Outside, Freya grabbed my arm. "Did you hear that? Your great-aunt called people the morning she died— including people on our mysterious list! She knew something was happening!"

"Or she was genuinely having chest pains and called friends for help," I countered, though I didn't believe it myself. "Either way, we're taking this to Drake now."

"Fine, but can we at least call Malcolm first? His name isn't on the list, but he was there that morning. He might know something crucial."

"No more delays. Police station first."

DI Drake was not in the station when we arrived, having been called to another incident, but Constable Peters assured us she'd return shortly. We waited in the sparse reception area, the list of names burning a hole in my pocket.

"Look who's here," a familiar voice observed. Elliot stood in the doorway, veterinary bag in hand. "Turning amateur detective work over to the professionals?"

"Something like that," I admitted. "What are you doing here?"

"Routine rabies vaccination paperwork for the station's new drug detection dog." He glanced at the folder I was clutching. "Found something significant, I take it?"

Before I could answer, the station door opened again, admitting DI Drake, whose expression shifted from professional neutrality to resigned recognition upon seeing us.

"Miss Hampton. Let me guess—you've discovered something you believe relates to the investigation?"

"Yes, actually." I stood, surprised by her perceptiveness.

"My office." She led the way down a short corridor, adding over her shoulder, "You too, Dr. Harrington, since you're clearly involved in whatever this is."

Elliot raised an eyebrow but followed without comment.

Drake's office was unexpectedly cluttered for someone so precise—case files stacked on every surface, a large whiteboard covered with notes and photographs, and three mugs of abandoned tea in various states of consumption.

"Right." She cleared space on a chair for me, ignoring Freya and Elliot who remained standing. "What have you found?"

I explained about the anonymous text and the hidden list, producing both my phone and the folded paper. "We

believe it relates to my great-aunt's death, not just Thornbury's murder."

Drake examined the list with methodical care, her
expression revealing nothing. "And you investigated before
bringing this to me because...?"

"We didn't—" I began.

"We talked to Mrs. Thatcher at the bakery," Freya interjected. "She told us Ginny's great-aunt called her the
morning she died, along with Malcolm from the bookshop.
Both said she complained of chest pains."

"Convenient symptoms for someone being poisoned,"
Elliot observed quietly.

Drake's gaze snapped to him. "Poisoned? That's quite an
accusation, Doctor."

"A medical observation, not an accusation." He remained
unruffled. "Certain toxins can present initially as cardiac
distress. Without specific testing, they're virtually unde-
tectable post mortem."

"Are you suggesting a medical examiner would miss
signs of poisoning?"

"I'm suggesting that without reason to suspect foul
play, standard protocols might not identify certain
substances. Particularly if the deceased had pre-existing
conditions that would make heart failure a reasonable
cause of death."

Drake's expression suggested reluctant agreement.
"You've given this some thought."

"I mentioned my concerns to Miss Hampton yesterday,"
he confirmed. "After hearing about the break-ins targeting
her great-aunt's research."

Drake turned back to me. "So we have a list of names, all
people who attended a fundraiser the day your great-aunt
died, sent to you anonymously." She tapped the paper

thoughtfully. "Did your great-aunt take medication regularly?"

The question caught me off guard. "I'm not sure. Probably? She was in her seventies."

"Prescription medication would be noted in her medical records." Drake made a note. "And would have been in her home."

"The cottage," I realized. "Someone broke in looking for something. What if it wasn't just research documents they wanted?"

"Medication that might have been tampered with," Elliot suggested. "Or emptied bottles that might contain trace evidence."

"This is all speculation," Drake cautioned, though she continued writing. "But worth exploring." She studied the three of us with a measuring look. "You realize you should have brought this to me immediately."

"We're bringing it now," I pointed out.

"After conducting your own inquiries." Her tone wasn't accusatory, just matter-of-fact. "Which, I might add, have yielded information my officers couldn't easily obtain. Mrs. Thatcher has been reluctant to speak with us about that morning."

"People talk differently to neighbors than to police," Elliot noted.

Drake nodded slowly. "Indeed. Which presents an... opportunity." She leaned forward. "Miss Hampton, would you be willing to continue gathering information—officially, as part of our investigation?"

"You want me to spy on my neighbors?" I was simultaneously appalled and intrigued.

"I want you to have conversations that would seem suspicious coming from officers but natural coming from a newcomer integrating into village life." She spread her hands. "You have access and connections we don't. Plus, you're already investigating, whether I approve or not."

"So you're deputizing her?" Freya looked thrilled by the prospect.

"Nothing so formal. Just a recognition that our investigations might be mutually beneficial." Drake's gaze returned to me. "With the understanding that you share everything you learn and take no unnecessary risks."

The offer was tempting. Official sanction for the investigating I was already doing, plus access to Drake's insights and resources.

"What about my friends?" I gestured to Freya and Elliot. "They're helping me."

Drake sighed. "Apparently I'm acquiring an entire amateur detective agency. Fine, but the same rules apply— share everything, no risks, and I retain full authority to shut down any line of inquiry that becomes dangerous."

"Agreed," I said, sensing this was as good an offer as we'd get.

"Good." She stood, signaling the end of our meeting. "Starting now, I want to know everyone your great-aunt contacted in her final days. Check phone records, emails, visitor logs at the shop. Find out who she trusted and who she feared."

As we filed out of her office, Drake added casually, "And Miss Hampton? Don't make me regret this arrangement."

Outside the station, Freya could barely contain her excitement. "We're official! Like Charlie's Angels, but with books!"

"We're confidential informants at best," Elliot corrected, though he seemed amused by her enthusiasm. "And Drake is hardly giving us free rein."

"Still, it's better than working against the police," I pointed out. "This way we share resources instead of duplicating efforts."

Elliot nodded. "Pragmatic of Drake. She recognizes that you'll investigate regardless, so she might as well channel your efforts productively."

"And get access to village gossip channels the police can't tap," Freya added. "Genius, really."

As we walked back toward the bookshop, I felt a curious mixture of validation and trepidation. Our unofficial investigation had just gained a veneer of officiality, but with it came increased responsibility. If we were wrong about my great-aunt's death, we'd be wasting police resources. If we were right, we were hunting a killer who had already struck twice and wouldn't hesitate to eliminate new threats.

"So," Freya asked as we reached the shop door, "what's our first official move as deputy detective bookshop owners?"

"We find out exactly what my great-aunt was researching before she died," I decided. "And who else knew about it."

The shop bell jangled as we entered, its cheerful sound at odds with our somber purpose. Whatever my great-aunt had discovered had likely cost her her life. The question was: would uncovering that truth cost us ours?

19

"I'd start with my great-aunt's appointment book," I told Freya as we prepared to open the shop. "If she was researching something dangerous, she might have recorded meetings or research sessions."

"Good thinking." Freya straightened a display with unusual focus. "But where would she keep it? We haven't found anything like that in the apartment."

"Malcolm might know. Speaking of whom, where is he?" I checked my watch. Five minutes past opening, and no sign of our punctual assistant manager.

"Maybe he's running late?" Freya suggested, though we both knew that was as likely as the King popping in for a browse.

I tried his mobile—straight to voicemail. Concerning, given yesterday's revelations about his presence when my great-aunt died.

"Should we be worried?" Freya asked, watching me frown at my phone.

"Maybe." I tried to sound casual. "Or maybe he just overslept."

The bell jangled, and we both turned expectantly, but it was Elspeth from the tea shop, not Malcolm.

"You're open!" she exclaimed with delight. "And I've brought proper breakfast—can't be expected to solve murders on an empty stomach." She deposited a basket of still-warm scones on the counter. It seemed they were the most popular baked goods. "The whole village is talking about your partnership with the police. So exciting!"

I blinked in confusion. "Our what?"

"Your detective arrangement! Constable Peters' wife told my cousin that DI Drake has officially brought you into the investigation. Quite unorthodox, but then, murder in Tidehaven Cove is hardly orthodox to begin with."

News traveled with alarming efficiency in this village. "It's not exactly a partnership," I clarified. "More of an information-sharing arrangement."

"Of course, dear." Elspeth winked conspiratorially. "Very hush-hush. I understand completely." Her stage whisper could probably be heard across the green. "I just wanted you to know that we're all behind you. Any assistance you need, just ask."

"Actually," Freya chimed in, "did you know Ginny's great-aunt well? We're trying to track down her appointment book or diary from her final months."

Elspeth's expression brightened further. "Investigating already! How splendid! Vivian always kept her schedule book in that lovely writing desk upstairs. The little mahogany one with the secret drawer."

"Secret drawer?" I repeated.

"In the right leg. Press the third carved rose and the panel slides out." She noticed our surprised expressions. "Oh, we all knew about it. Vivian would hide birthday presents for the staff there. Not much of a secret in a village this size."

After Elspeth departed, promising to return with lunch and "any useful gossip", Freya and I exchanged looks.

"Secret drawer?" she whispered. "How did we miss that?"

"Let's find out." I headed for the stairs, Freya close behind.

The writing desk sat in the corner of the apartment's living room—a delicate piece with solid legs and inlaid woods. I examined the right leg, finding the carved roses Elspeth had mentioned. Sure enough, pressing the third one released a small, hidden drawer that slid out smoothly from the side.

Inside lay a leather-bound appointment book and a small brass key.

"The key from the break-in," Freya gasped. "It matches this one!"

She was right. The police had found an identical key with a ship's wheel design.

"Two keys to the same lock," I mused. "One for my great-aunt, one for..."

"Whoever broke in looking for whatever these unlock," Freya finished.

I set the key aside and opened the appointment book. The final entries were dated mid-April, stopping abruptly on the 14th—the day before my great-aunt died. Most notations were routine bookshop matters, but certain entries were marked with a small star, including several meetings with "R.T." and "N.P."

"Reginald Thornbury and Nathaniel Penrose," I translated. "She was meeting with both of them regularly in her final weeks."

"What about these?" Freya pointed to entries marked "M.B. - archive review."

"Malcolm Blackwood. Looks like they were systematically going through the shop's archives." I flipped back through earlier months. "Starting in January, right after Victoria Ashford purchased Tidehaven Manor."

"Coincidence?" The way she said it didn't leave much room to pretend otherwise.

"I doubt it," I murmured, turning to the final page. The last entry, dated April 14th, read: *Insurance documentation completed. Files secured. M.B. still objects, but necessity overrides caution.*

"Insurance documentation," I repeated. "Just like in her journal—she mentioned making copies as 'insurance.'"

"And Malcolm objected," Freya noted. "To what, exactly?"

"To revealing the truth about the Ashford family, presumably." I closed the book. "We need to find Malcolm. His absence now seems even more suspicious."

Before we could formulate a plan, the shop bell jangled again. This time it was Elliot, expression serious as he approached the counter.

"Have you seen the morning paper?" he asked without preamble, placing a folded newspaper before us.

The headline read: *HISTORICAL SOCIETY TREASURER FOUND DEAD – POLICE INVESTIGATE POSSIBLE CONNECTION TO BOOKSHOP MURDER*

"Gerald Winters," Elliot explained, seeing my confusion. "Local accountant and historical society treasurer. Found this morning in his home office. 'Apparent suicide,' according to initial reports."

I scanned the article with growing dread. Gerald Winters, 68, had been discovered by his housekeeper, slumped over his desk with an empty whiskey bottle and what appeared to be a suicide note expressing remorse for "past mistakes coming to light."

"Gerald Winters," I repeated, a chill running down my spine. "He's on the list we found."

"And conveniently dead before the police could question him about your great-aunt," Elliot observed grimly.

"You think it's connected?" Freya asked.

"Two deaths linked to the historical society within days of a murder involving historical documents?" Elliot raised an eyebrow. "Either that's remarkable coincidence, or someone is eliminating loose ends."

I reached for my phone. "I'm calling DI Drake."

Twenty minutes later, we were back at the police station, the appointment book and brass key secured in evidence bags as Drake questioned us in her office.

"Gerald Winters was the historical society's treasurer for fifteen years," she confirmed. "He would have handled the finances for their archives, including acquisitions like the Harbormaster's Journal."

"Was it suicide?" I asked bluntly.

Drake's expression remained neutral. "We're investigating all possibilities. The scene was... suspiciously perfect. Like something from detective fiction rather than real life."

"Staged," Elliot translated.

"Potentially," she conceded. "Though the handwriting on the note appears authentic. We're waiting on toxicology results."

"Just like you should be doing for my great-aunt," I pressed. Was her death on the back burner? Did the authorities think hers wasn't connected?

"Already ordered this morning, along with exhumation

paperwork." Her direct acknowledgment surprised me. "Your information about her connections to Thornbury's research and the timing of her death created sufficient grounds for review."

"Thank you," I said, genuinely grateful.

"Don't thank me yet. Exhumation requires family permission—that's you—and a judge's order, which takes time." She tapped her pen against the appointment book. "Meanwhile, this creates new avenues of investigation. We need to track every starred meeting in the weeks before her death."

"And find Malcolm," I added. "He's missing, and apparently he objected to whatever 'insurance documentation' my great-aunt was creating."

Drake frowned. "Objected how?"

I couldn't wait for her to read the pages. Perhaps an objection wasn't and indication of foul play, but it was something."We don't know specifically. But he was there at the cottage, supposedly arriving just as emergency services were taking her away."

"Having missed her call for help because he was supposedly in the bookshop basement," Freya added.

"That's not in the official report," Drake said, checking a file. "According to this, Malcolm Blackwood arrived after police were already on scene."

"But Mrs. Thatcher said—"

"That he claimed to have missed a call from Vivian because he was shelving books," Drake finished with a nod. "Interesting discrepancy."

The implications hung in the air. Malcolm had lied—either to Mrs. Thatcher about receiving a call, or to the police about when he arrived.

"We need to find him," Drake stated firmly. "I'll have officers check his residence. You two," she nodded to Freya and me, "check anywhere in the village he might frequent. Discreetly."

"What about the key?" I asked. "It matches one found at the break-in scene."

"Likely opens something in the bookshop, given its location and your great-aunt's profession." Drake handed me a slip of paper. "This is my direct number. Call immediately if you find Malcolm or determine what those keys might unlock."

Back at the bookshop, we found a small queue of customers waiting—apparently news of our "detective partnership" had boosted business even further.

"Everyone wants to talk to the bookshop sleuths," Freya whispered as we unlocked the door. "Should we use this to our advantage?"

"Absolutely," I decided. "But subtly. Ask about Malcolm —casually, like we're just wondering where he is."

Throughout the morning, we worked this approach with every customer. Most knew Malcolm only as the proper bookseller who could locate any volume in seconds, but a few offered more useful information.

"Saw him at the church yesterday evening," reported Dot, who'd come in for another gardening book. "Standing by the memorial garden, looking troubled. Not that Malcolm ever looks particularly cheerful, mind you, but distinct storm clouds yesterday."

"The church memorial garden?" I repeated. "Is that significant?"

"It's where your great-aunt's ashes are interred," Dot explained. "Malcolm visits weekly with fresh flowers. Very devoted, he is."

This added another dimension to Malcolm's relationship with my great-aunt. Not just professional loyalty, but perhaps deeper affection.

By lunchtime, we had several potential Malcolm sightings but no concrete leads. I was considering closing early to expand our search when the shop door opened and DI Drake entered, looking grimmer than usual.

"We found Malcolm Blackwood," she announced without preamble. "He's in hospital. Apparent overdose of sleeping medication. Found in his flat by his landlady when she came to investigate water leaking into the downstairs apartment."

"Is he..." I couldn't finish the question.

"Alive, but unconscious. Doctors are cautiously optimistic." Drake's expression softened slightly. "His landlady said his flat was in disarray—not consistent with Malcolm's usual meticulous habits. We're treating it as suspicious."

Another convenient "suicide attempt" from someone connected to my great-aunt's research. The pattern was becoming impossible to ignore.

"There was a note," Drake continued. "Not a suicide note, but a letter addressed to you, Miss Hampton. Found on his desk, apparently interrupted mid-writing."

She handed me a plastic evidence bag containing a sheet of stationery with Malcolm's precise handwriting.

Miss Hampton,

I must confess my grave error in judgment. Your great-aunt entrusted me with protecting the truth, and I have failed through misplaced loyalty. The Harbormaster's Journal was only part of the evidence. The rest is hidden where water meets land, guarded by the blind captain. I should have told you immediately, but old obligations clouded my judgment.

Victoria Ashford is not what she seems. Her interest in Tide-

haven Cove's history is not preservation but erasure. I believe she
was responsible for your great-aunt's

The letter ended abruptly, as if Malcolm had been interrupted while writing.

"Where water meets land, guarded by the blind captain," Freya repeated. "What does that mean?"

"A riddle? A code?" I looked to Drake. "Has forensics examined his flat? Were there signs of forced entry?"

"No obvious evidence of intrusion, but the investigation is ongoing. His medication appears to have been in his evening tea—much more concentrated in the dregs than would be expected from his regular dose of tablets."

"Someone put it in his tea," Elliot concluded, having joined us from the veterinary clinic after receiving my text. "Just like they may have done with Vivian Hampton's heart medication."

Drake nodded grimly. "Two apparent suicides and a murder, all connected to historical research about the Ashford family. We're beyond coincidence now."

"What about the riddle?" I pressed. "Water meets land, blind captain?"

"Could be the harbor," Freya suggested. "Water meets land there."

"But what's the 'blind captain'?" Elliot mused.

As if summoned by the question, a gray shape leapt onto the sales counter. Captain the cat sat with imperial dignity, his battle-scarred face regarding us with his one good eye— the other a permanently closed scar.

"The blind captain," I breathed. "Not blind, but missing an eye. Captain the cat!"

"You think your assistant hid crucial evidence with a stray cat?" Drake looked skeptical.

"Not with. Near." I studied Captain's unimpressed

expression. "My great-aunt fed him by the garden shed —'where water meets land' could mean the stream at the bottom of the cottage garden. It borders the property where the shed is located."

Drake's skepticism remained, but she nodded. "Worth investigating. But not alone," she added firmly. "I'll arrange officers to accompany us. Meanwhile, I want the shop closed and you three somewhere secure. If someone is eliminating everyone connected to this research, you're all potential targets."

"You can both stay at my place," Elliot offered. "It's outside the village, private drive, good visibility from all approaches."

"Acceptable," Drake agreed before I could respond. "Pack essentials only. I'll have an officer escort you there while I arrange a team for the cottage search."

As Drake made calls, I gathered necessities from the apartment, trying to process these rapid developments. Malcolm poisoned. Another historical society member dead. A cryptic message about hidden evidence.

Whatever my great-aunt had discovered about the Ashford family wasn't just scandalous history—it was dangerous present-day truth with deadly consequences. And now we were fully enmeshed in the investigation, moving from amateur consultation to potential targets.

"Ready?" Freya appeared in the doorway, overnight bag in hand, expression uncharacteristically serious.

"As I'll ever be." I zipped my bag and gathered the dogs' leashes. "Did you see where Captain went?"

"He disappeared when Drake started making calls. Probably back to whatever secret evidence stash he's guarding."

I smiled despite everything. "Let's hope he leads us to it before anyone else finds it."

"Spoken like a true detective," Freya approved.

I wasn't sure if that was a compliment or a concern. Either way, there was no turning back now. We were officially in the investigation—and potentially in the killer's crosshairs.

lliot's home proved to be not the rustic cottage I'd imagined, but a surprising blend of traditional and modern—a stone farmhouse that had been thoughtfully renovated with clean lines and abundant natural light. It sat nestled against a hillside with views across rolling pastures to the distant sea, isolated enough for privacy but not so remote as to feel abandoned.

"This is your house?" Freya voiced my surprise as we followed Elliot up the gravel drive, a police cruiser trailing behind us. "It's gorgeous!"

"Family property," he explained, unlocking the front door. "My grandfather's originally. I've updated it over the years."

Inside was equally impressive—open spaces, comfortable furnishings, and walls lined with bookshelves. A sleek modern kitchen opened onto a living area anchored by a substantial stone fireplace. The effect was welcoming rather than showy, the home of someone with good taste and the means to indulge it without ostentation.

"Make yourselves comfortable," Elliot gestured toward

the guest rooms off a central hallway. "There's plenty of space."

While Freya explored with unabashed curiosity, I checked my phone for updates from Drake. Nothing yet. The waiting was already excruciating, and we'd barely begun.

"They'll call when they find something," Elliot said, noting my fixation on the screen. "Drake seems thorough."

"She is," I agreed. "I'm just not good at sitting around waiting."

"Then we should continue the investigation." He moved to the kitchen and began filling a kettle. "Think about what we know so far. Make connections. That's what your great-aunt would do."

He was right. I found paper and pen in a drawer he indicated and began listing facts while Elliot prepared tea and Freya continued her self-guided tour, exclaiming occasionally over some new discovery.

"The historical society fundraiser was April 14," I began, writing as I spoke. "Victoria Ashford hosted it at the manor —her first major public event after moving to Tidehaven Cove."

"Establishing herself as a preservation champion," Elliot noted, setting mugs on the counter. "Perfect cover for someone actually interested in suppressing history."

"Gerald Winters was the society's treasurer. He handled their finances, including acquisitions like the Harbormaster's Journal." I added his name to the growing diagram. "He's now conveniently dead of apparent suicide."

"Along with Malcolm's suspicious overdose," Elliot added. "Both potentially silenced before they could reveal what they knew."

"My great-aunt made 'insurance documentation' that

Malcolm initially objected to. She hid it somewhere near water, possibly by the stream at the bottom of the cottage garden." I circled this point several times. "And Captain the cat somehow factors in."

"Cats are territorial," Elliot observed, pouring the tea. "If your great-aunt fed him regularly in a specific location, he would consider that spot his domain."

"Like the garden shed?" I recalled how the cat had appeared during the break-in's aftermath. "Maybe he was guarding it all along."

"Or somewhere nearby." Elliot handed me a steaming mug. "The stream forms a natural boundary at the bottom of several properties. Is there anything distinctive about that area?"

I tried to visualize the cottage garden. "There's an old stone wall along the stream bank. Some kind of former mill structure, according to Dot. And a small footbridge."

"Any of which could conceal hidden documents," Elliot concluded.

Freya rejoined us, her exploration complete. "This place is amazing! There's a whole veterinary reference library upstairs." She accepted the tea Elliot offered. "Any updates from Drake?"

"Not yet." I showed her my notes. "We're thinking about where the 'blind captain' might guard something."

"Wait," Freya held up her phone. "I just found this." She turned the screen to show us a village heritage website with a page titled 'Tidehaven Cove's Maritime Connections.' "There's a stone marker by the stream—originally a mooring post when the stream was wider centuries ago. Local kids call it 'Captain's Watch.'"

"Where water meets land," I breathed. "And if erosion or vegetation has damaged the carved face..."

"A blind captain," Elliot finished.

I was already calling Drake. She answered on the first ring. "We're at the cottage now. Nothing significant in the garden shed beyond what forensics already cataloged."

"Check the stream boundary," I said without preamble. "There's an old mooring post called Captain's Watch. It might be what Malcolm meant by the blind captain."

There was a brief silence, then: "Constable Peters, take two officers to the stream boundary. Look for a stone marker or mooring post." To me, she added, "How did you figure this out?"

"Research and local knowledge," I replied. "Any word on Malcolm's condition?"

"Still unconscious but stable. Doctors are more optimistic now." A pause, then Drake's voice grew distant as she directed officers. When she returned to the phone, her tone had changed. "We'll update you when we find anything. Stay secure."

The call ended abruptly, leaving me frustrated. "They're checking the stream now."

"And we wait," Freya sighed dramatically. "I hate waiting."

"I have a distraction," Elliot offered. "Since we're stuck here, why not review what we know about the Ashford family? I have some local history books that might help."

Anything was better than staring at our phones. Soon we were surrounded by volumes on Devon maritime history and old maps of the coastline. Elliot's collection was surprisingly comprehensive.

"Professional interest," he explained, noting my raised eyebrow. "Animal husbandry practices evolved alongside shipping and trade. The histories are intertwined."

We lost ourselves in research, piecing together fragments of the Ashford family history. Their shipping company had indeed been hugely profitable until a sudden decline in the mid-1840s. References to a "scandal" appeared in several texts but without specifics.

"It's like there's a deliberate gap in the historical record," Freya noted, comparing sources. "Everyone acknowledges something happened, but the details are conspicuously absent."

"Historical sanitization," Elliot suggested. "Powerful families could influence what was recorded, especially regarding embarrassing incidents."

"But my great-aunt found evidence that couldn't be sanitized," I said. "The Harbormaster's Journal and whatever supporting documentation Malcolm hid."

My phone vibrated suddenly—a text from Drake: *Found something. Sending officer to transport you to station. 30 min.*

"They found it," I announced, showing them the message. "Whatever Malcolm hid, they've got it."

"Or they found something else entirely," Elliot cautioned. "Don't jump to conclusions."

He was right to be wary. This entire investigation had been a series of false leads and unexpected turns. But the prospect of concrete evidence was too tantalizing to dismiss.

We gathered our things and waited by the front window, watching for the promised police transport. The afternoon sun was beginning its descent, casting long shadows across Elliot's garden. Despite the comfortable surroundings, tension thrummed through me like an electric current.

"What do you think they found?" Freya asked, breaking the silence.

"Hopefully the 'insurance documentation' my great-aunt mentioned," I replied. "Something substantial enough to justify three deaths."

"More," Elliot corrected quietly. "If your great-aunt was indeed murdered, she won't be the first to get too close to the truth."

The weight of that possibility had been growing steadily in my mind. Not just Thornbury and the others, but my own flesh and blood—killed to protect a historical secret.

A car appeared on the winding drive, but not the expected police cruiser. Instead, a sleek black BMW crawled toward the house, its approach deliberate and unhurried.

"That's Victoria Ashford's car," I realized with a chill.

Elliot moved immediately to a drawer, extracting what appeared to be a small security device. "Stay away from the windows." His tone was calm but commanding. "Freya, take the dogs to the back bedroom. Ginny, call Drake."

I dialed with shaking fingers while Elliot activated some kind of alarm system I hadn't noticed before. Drake answered immediately. "We're still processing the scene. The officer should be there shortly."

"Victoria Ashford is here," I said quietly. "At Elliot's house. Right now."

A beat of silence. "Are you certain?"

"Her BMW is coming up the drive. We're not expecting anyone else."

"Lock all doors and windows. Stay away from entrances. Officers are being dispatched now." Drake's professional composure slipped slightly. "How did she know your location?"

It was the question hammering through my own mind. Our relocation had been arranged hastily but discreetly. Unless...

"Someone at the station must have told her," I realized. "Or she followed us."

"Stay on the line," Drake instructed. "Assistance is coming."

The BMW stopped in front of the house. Through a gap in the curtains, I could see Victoria emerge, looking as polished and composed as ever in a camel coat and leather gloves. She walked to the trunk, opened it, and removed something I couldn't quite see.

"She's got something from her trunk," I reported. "I can't tell what."

"Is she armed?" Drake's voice was tense, but I could tell she was on the move.

"I don't know. She's coming to the front door now."

The doorbell rang, its cheerful chime incongruously normal in the tense atmosphere. None of us moved.

"Miss Hampton?" Victoria's voice called through the door. "I know you're in there. I've brought something I think you'll find interesting."

The doorbell rang again, more insistently.

"Really, this is childish," Victoria continued. "I'm trying to help. The police are making a terrible mistake, and I have documentation to prove it."

I covered the phone's microphone. "What if she really does have information?"

"Then she can provide it through proper channels," Elliot replied firmly. "Not by tracking you to a secure location."

The doorbell stopped. For a moment, I thought she'd given up, but then her voice came again, closer to a window this time.

"I understand your caution. I'll leave the file here on the step. Review it when you're ready. It explains everything about your great-aunt's research—and why Malcolm Blackwood tried to kill himself."

A car door slammed, and the BMW's engine started. Through the gap in the curtains, I watched Victoria drive away, her departure as unhurried as her arrival.

"She's leaving," I told Drake. "Said she left a file on the doorstep about my great-aunt's research."

"Do not open that door," Drake ordered. "It could be a trap. Wait for my officers."

Five minutes later, a police cruiser roared up the drive, two uniformed officers approaching the house with tactical caution. After a thorough examination, one retrieved a manila envelope from the doorstep while the other secured the perimeter.

"All clear, ma'am," the senior officer reported after checking the envelope for obvious hazards. "Just papers inside. We'll take you to the station now, where DI Drake is waiting."

The drive to the station passed in tense silence. None of us knew quite what to make of Victoria's strange visit or the envelope now secured in an evidence bag between us.

At the station, Drake met us in the conference room, her expression grave. "We found documentation hidden in a waterproof container beneath the stone mooring post. Historical records, shipping manifests, and personal correspondence dating to the 1840s." She placed a file folder on the table. "Along with this."

Inside was a typed document titled "Final Statement of Vivian Hampton-Davies" and dated April 14, 2020. Quite possibly the last thing she wrote.

"My great-aunt's statement," I whispered.

"Her insurance," Drake confirmed. "A detailed account of what she discovered about the Ashford family's involvement in falsifying inheritance and genealogy, complete with supporting evidence and witness testimonies." She met my eyes directly. "And her suspicion that Victoria Ashford returned to Tidehaven Cove specifically to locate and destroy this evidence."

"Which is why Victoria just tried to deliver her own counter-evidence," Elliot concluded.

"Presumably," Drake agreed. "Though I wouldn't trust anything from that source. Our forensics team is examining her envelope now."

"So what happens next?" I asked, still processing the confirmation that my great-aunt had indeed been investigating exactly what we suspected. "And why would these papers resurfacing be enough to kill?"

"Families could lose everything," Elliot said. "I suppose it's difficult for a American to grasp. Most of the land grants and licenses came from the monarch in those days. Falsifying them is treason. There is no statute of limitations on that."

"Next, we review all evidence, including whatever Victoria Ashford provided. We continue investigating the suspicious deaths. And," Drake added with unusual gentleness, "we await toxicology results from your great-aunt's exhumation, which was completed this afternoon."

The reality of that process—my great-aunt's remains being scientifically examined—hit me with unexpected force. This wasn't just an intellectual puzzle anymore. It was personal, visceral, and increasingly dangerous.

"In the meantime," Drake continued, "you'll remain under police protection. The cottage and bookshop are still potential crime scenes, so alternative accommodation will be necessary."

"They can continue staying with me," Elliot offered. "My property is isolated and secure."

Drake nodded approval. "With additional officers

stationed nearby. Victoria Ashford's unusual approach today suggests escalation—a dangerous new phase in whatever game she's playing."

As arrangements were finalized, I found myself staring at my great-aunt's final statement, its pages carefully preserved in plastic sleeves. She had known the risks of her investigation. Had prepared for the worst. Had created "insurance" against those who would suppress the truth.

And now that insurance had passed to me—along with all the danger it entailed.

21

The morning brought news that changed everything. Drake called while we were having breakfast at Elliot's kitchen table, her voice tight with controlled urgency.

"Toxicology results are in," she announced without preamble. "Your great-aunt was poisoned. Digitalis— foxglove extract—administered in sufficient quantity to trigger fatal cardiac arrhythmia."

I set down my coffee cup with trembling hands. "So she was murdered."

"Without question. The concentration was far beyond what could occur naturally or accidentally." Drake's tone softened slightly. "I'm sorry, Ginny. I know this confirms your worst fears."

"It also means we're hunting a killer," I said, surprised by how steady my voice sounded. "What about Malcolm?"

"Similar findings. Digitalis combined with the sleeping medication—a lethal cocktail disguised as suicide." Papers rustled in the background. "Gerald Winters showed traces as well, though the concentration was lower. He may have realized what was happening and fought back."

Freya reached across the table to squeeze my hand. "At least now we have proof someone's systematically eliminating people."

"Proof of method, yes. But we still need to establish who had access to poison all three victims." Drake paused. "However, we've had a breakthrough on that front. The historical society's tea service from the fundraiser."

"What about it?" Elliot asked, leaning closer to the phone.

"Every victim attended that fundraiser on April 14th. We've located the caterer who provided the refreshments—Mrs. Bellweather from the next village over. She's been very cooperative about her procedures that night."

My pulse quickened. "And?"

"She brought all the tea service, but the hostess—Victoria Ashford—insisted on preparing the actual tea herself. Said it was a family tradition, something about proper steeping techniques passed down through generations." Drake's satisfaction was audible. "Mrs. Bellweather thought it was odd but didn't want to offend her new client."

"So Victoria had access to everyone's tea that night," I breathed.

"More than that. Mrs. Bellweather specifically remembers Victoria asking detailed questions about who preferred which types of tea. She made a point of serving people personally, ensuring everyone got 'exactly what they liked.'"

"She was targeting specific people even then," Freya said with dawning horror. "Not random poisoning—carefully selected victims."

"It appears so. We're testing the remaining tea service now, though after three months, we may not find residue."

Drake's tone became businesslike. "But we have something else. Victoria made a mistake."

"What kind of mistake?"

"When she delivered that envelope to Dr. Harrington's house, she used her car's GPS navigation system. We've obtained the device records with a warrant." The satisfaction in Drake's voice was unmistakable. "The GPS shows multiple trips to locations connected to our investigation—including your cottage on both nights it was broken into."

My blood chilled. "She was stalking me from the beginning."

"Monitoring your movements, yes. The GPS data shows she drove past your cottage at least a dozen times in the days after Thornbury's murder. She also made several trips to Malcolm's flat in the days before his poisoning."

"That's pretty damning evidence," Elliot observed.

"Combined with the toxicology results and witness testimony about the tea service, yes. We have enough for an arrest warrant." Drake paused. "There's just one problem."

"Which is?"

"Victoria Ashford has disappeared. Her car was found abandoned at Exeter train station this morning. We've alerted all ports and airports, but she had a significant head start."

The news hit like a physical blow. After everything we'd endured—the murders, the break-ins, the constant fear—our killer had simply vanished.

"How long has she been gone?" I asked.

"Her housekeeper says she didn't come home last night. The car was abandoned sometime before dawn, based on parking enforcement records." Drake's frustration was evident. "We're treating it as a flight to avoid prosecution."

"Or she's planning something else," I said, voicing the

fear that had immediately sprung to mind. "Something final."

"We've increased security around all potential targets," Drake assured me. "You, Malcolm, Dr. Penrose—anyone connected to the investigation."

"What about the bookshop? If she's desperate enough to run, she might try to destroy the evidence we found."

"Already considered. We have officers stationed there around the clock." Drake's tone became gentler. "Ginny, I know this is frustrating, but sometimes the best we can do is make ourselves hard to find targets and wait for the fugitive to make a mistake."

After the call ended, we sat in contemplative silence. The confirmation of murder felt both vindicating and terrifying—proof that our instincts were correct, but also that we'd been in genuine danger all along.

"She could be anywhere by now," Freya said finally. "London, Europe, anywhere with an airport."

"Maybe," Elliot said thoughtfully. "But she's spent the last six months establishing herself in Tidehaven Cove. Her whole identity as a heritage preservationist was built around this place. Would she really just abandon it?"

"If the alternative is life in prison, yes," I replied. "Though you raise a good point about her investment here. She bought Tidehaven Manor, renovated it, joined the historical society..."

"Established an entire false identity," Freya added. "That takes commitment. And time. And money."

"It also takes desperation," I pointed out. "She killed three people to protect whatever secret she's hiding. That's not rational behavior."

My phone buzzed with a text from an unknown number: *The truth about your great-aunt's research is more dangerous than you know. Meet me at Tidehaven Manor at 2 PM if you want to understand why people had to die. Come alone. -V.A.*

I showed the message to the others, watching their expressions shift from surprise to alarm.

"She's still here," Elliot said grimly. "And she's not done."

"Absolutely not," Freya said immediately. "It must be a trap."

"Or a desperate attempt to justify her actions," I countered, though my pulse had quickened at the implications. "She knows we have the evidence. Maybe she wants to explain her side before she disappears forever."

"Or eliminate the final witnesses," Elliot pointed out. "You can't seriously be considering this."

I wasn't sure what I was considering. The rational part of my mind recognized the danger, but something else—curiosity, anger, or perhaps inherited stubbornness—made me reluctant to dismiss the opportunity entirely.

"I'm calling Drake," I announced.

Drake's response was predictably direct: "Under no circumstances. We have units moving toward the manor now because we assessed it as a probable hiding place. Victoria Ashford is not to be approached by civilians."

"But what if she has information about other potential victims?" I pressed. "Or evidence we haven't found?"

"Then she can provide it through proper legal channels after her arrest." Drake's tone brooked no argument. "Your safety is the priority now, not satisfying curiosity."

Despite her clear instructions, I found myself thinking about the message throughout the morning. What truth could be "more dangerous than we knew"? And why risk exposure by proposing a meeting when she must know the police were closing in?

By early afternoon, the question had evolved into an itch

I couldn't quite scratch. Elliot had gone to check on a patient emergency, leaving Freya and me with the patrol officers stationed discreetly around the property. Tidehaven Manor was visible from Elliot's upper windows—a grand house set in landscaped grounds about half a mile away.

"You're thinking about it," Freya observed, noting my frequent glances toward the manor. "I can practically see the gears turning."

"I'm thinking about what my great-aunt would do," I admitted. "She investigated dangerous truths even when it put her at risk."

"And look what happened to her," Freya pointed out with uncharacteristic bluntness. "Victoria Ashford is a killer, Ginny. Multiple times over. Meeting her alone would be suicide."

"But what if she's ready to confess? What if this is her attempt to finally tell the truth?" I turned from the window to face Freya directly. "My great-aunt died because someone wanted to suppress historical facts. Shouldn't we at least try to understand what was worth killing for?"

"We should let the police handle it," Freya replied firmly. "They're trained for dangerous situations. We run a bookshop."

She was right, of course. But as 2 PM approached, my restlessness increased. Through the binoculars Elliot kept for birdwatching, I could see police cars positioned around the manor's perimeter, but no sign of activity from the house itself.

At exactly 2 PM, my phone rang. Unknown number.

"Miss Hampton." Victoria's voice was calmer than I expected, almost conversational. "I see you decided not to join me. Disappointing, but understandable given the police presence."

"They'll arrest you if you try to leave," I warned.

"Will they? I rather think they'll be too busy with other concerns shortly." A hint of something—amusement? desperation?—crept into her tone. "I have something I think you should know before this all ends."

"Then tell me now."

"The documents your great-aunt found weren't just about my family's falsified land grants, Ginny. They implicate dozens of prominent Devon families—MPs, magistrates, major landowners. All built on the same forged medieval charters from the 1840s."

There were definite hints about multiple conspirators, but the scope she was suggesting seemed excessive. "That's a serious accusation, but hardly worth multiple murders."

"Isn't it? When those families control most of the county's wealth and political power?" Victoria's voice carried a note of desperation now. "Your great-aunt found evidence of a conspiracy involving half the Devon gentry. Land worth billions, parliamentary seats, judicial positions—all illegitimate."

Something in her tone didn't ring true. "You're exaggerating to scare me off."

"Am I? Do you really think my family acted alone in the 1840s? Do you think we were the only ones who saw an opportunity to improve our fortunes through creative documentation?" Her voice grew more frantic. "This evidence would destroy everyone from the Lord Lieutenant down to the village magistrate. They'll do anything to stop it— including eliminating one American bookshop owner who doesn't understand the stakes."

The line went quiet for a moment, then Victoria continued more softly. "Your great-aunt was naive, Ginny.

She thought truth was always worth the cost. But some truths are too dangerous for civilization to bear."

Before I could respond, the call ended. Through the binoculars, I could see smoke beginning to rise from the manor.

22

"Fire at Tidehaven Manor!" I called to Freya, dropping the binoculars as smoke billowed from the grand house's upper windows. "She's burning evidence!"

We rushed outside to find the patrol officers already coordinating emergency response. Fire engines wailed in the distance as police cars raced toward the manor, their sirens creating a cacophony that echoed across the peaceful Devon countryside.

"Stay here," the senior officer instructed firmly. "This is an active situation with a dangerous suspect."

But within minutes, it became clear the fire was contained to a small section of the manor—deliberate and controlled rather than destructive. Through Elliot's binoculars, we could see Victoria standing calmly in the front garden, watching the flames with an expression of grim satisfaction. The sirens still in the distance didn't hold her attention at all.

My phone rang again.

"It's done," Victoria announced without preamble. "The

documents that would have destroyed so many lives are gone. Reduced to ash."

"The police already have copies," I reminded her. "You've accomplished nothing except making yourself look more guilty."

"Have they?" Her voice carried a note of triumph. "I rather think they have copies of what I wanted them to find. The real evidence—the insurance documents your great-aunt created—were hidden much more cleverly."

A chill ran down my spine. "What do you mean?"

"Your great-aunt was paranoid, Ginny. Understandably so, given what she'd discovered. She didn't trust banks or safety deposit boxes or even her precious garden shed." Victoria's tone became almost conversational. "She hid the most damaging evidence in the one place she knew it would be safe from people like me."

"Where?"

"Inside books, of course. Hollowed out volumes in her own shop, scattered throughout the collection where only someone who truly knew her system could find them." The satisfaction in her voice was chilling. "I've spent months searching, but there are thousands of books in that shop. I needed someone with intimate knowledge of her cataloging methods."

"Malcolm," I breathed.

"Poor Malcolm. So devoted, so protective. He genuinely didn't understand what he was protecting when he refused to help me. Even when I explained how many innocent people would suffer if the truth came out."

"So you poisoned him."

"I gave him what I thought was a fatal dose, yes. His survival was... inconvenient. But not insurmountable." Her voice hardened. "He's told you where to find them, hasn't he? The real documents?"

I thought of Malcolm's cryptic message about *where water meets land, guarded by the blind captain.* We'd assumed it referred to the cottage garden, but what if he'd meant something else entirely?

"I don't know what you're talking about," I said, trying to keep my voice steady.

"Of course you do. Malcolm left you clues—he's far too honorable to take such secrets to his grave. The question is whether you're clever enough to solve them." Victoria paused. "And whether you'll be alive long enough to act on them."

The line went dead. Through the binoculars, I could see Victoria walking calmly toward a car that wasn't hers—a dark sedan with two figures inside.

"She's not alone," I realized with growing alarm. "Someone's helping her."

Freya grabbed the binoculars. "I can't see the other people clearly, but they're driving away from the police. Victoria's in the passenger seat."

My phone buzzed with another text: *Your great-aunt's real insurance is still hidden. Find it before I find you. You have until midnight. -V.A.*

"We need to call Drake," Freya said immediately.

But when I tried, the call went straight to voicemail. The emergency response at the manor was consuming all available resources, leaving us essentially on our own to decipher Malcolm's message.

"Where water meets land," I repeated, pacing Elliot's kitchen. "We thought it meant the cottage garden stream, but what if it's more metaphorical?"

"Like what?" Freya asked, making tea with mechanical

precision—a British response to crisis that I was beginning to appreciate.

"What if it's about the bookshop itself? The shop is on the corner where two streets meet—Bookshop Row and Market Street. The street names have changed over the years, haven't they?" I asked as a memory floated into focus from my research. "Wasn't Bookshop Row once called Neptune's run?"

Freya's eyes widened. "Yes, some religious group changed it in the forties claiming it venerated a heathen god. So, Neptune and Market. Like water flowing together. Brilliant. What about the blind captain?"

I thought about Captain the cat's distinctive appearance. "Captain has one eye, but he's not really blind. What if Malcolm meant something that looks like it can't see but actually can?"

"A window display?" Freya suggested, scratching at her mess of bun as if to stimulate her mind. "Books arranged so they look decorative but actually contain hidden documents?"

"Or something nautical—remember, the Harbormaster's Journal was the key to everything. My great-aunt specialized in maritime history."

Freya's eyes lit up. "The compass! The big brass compass in the shop's maritime section. It's been there so long everyone forgets it's actually functional."

"A compass shows direction—it 'sees' magnetic north even when it looks like just decoration." I felt pieces clicking together. "And it's in the section my great-aunt curated personally."

"We should wait for the police," Freya said, though she was already gathering her things.

"Victoria said we have until midnight. That's less than

ten hours, and she obviously has help now—people who might be watching the bookshop." I made the decision that felt both reckless and inevitable. "We need to check before she realizes what Malcolm meant."

Twenty minutes later, we stood outside Hampton Books, the village eerily quiet except for distant sirens still echoing from the manor. The shop looked peaceful in the afternoon light, but I couldn't shake the feeling we were being watched.

"The police tape's been removed from the main floor," Freya observed as I unlocked the door. "At least we won't be contaminating a crime scene."

Inside, the familiar smell of books and wood polish was reassuring. Austen and Hardy, who'd insisted on accompanying us despite my worries, immediately began their customary exploration while we headed for the maritime history section.

The brass compass sat exactly where it had for years—a substantial piece mounted on a wooden base, surrounded by books on navigation and seamanship. It looked purely decorative, but when I examined it more closely, I noticed something odd.

"The base is hollow," I realized, running my fingers around the edges. "And there's a seam here, like it opens."

"How do you open it?" Freya peered over my shoulder.

I tried twisting, lifting, and pressing various parts of the compass with no success. Then I remembered Malcolm's precise nature and his love of proper procedures.

"What if you have to set it to a specific bearing first?" I suggested, carefully rotating the compass needle. "Malcolm would appreciate the elegance of using a navigation instrument properly."

"What bearing, though?"

I thought about the clues Malcolm had left, about my great-aunt's methodical nature, about the central mystery that had started everything. "The Maria Constance sank off the Devon coast. What if the compass needs to point toward the wreck site?"

Working from memory of the old charts we'd studied, I carefully adjusted the compass to point southwest toward the area where the ship had gone down. As the needle settled into position, I heard a soft click.

The wooden base opened like a puzzle box, revealing a hidden compartment containing several waterproof packets.

"Malcolm, you brilliant man," I breathed, carefully extracting the packets. "He used the compass as both hiding place and puzzle."

Inside the packets were photocopies of documents I'd never seen—correspondence between Victorian officials, bank records, property transfers, and most importantly, a detailed analysis of everything written in my great-aunt's handwriting.

"This is it," I said, reading quickly. "The real evidence. Not just about the Ashford family, but about the network of officials who helped cover up the document forgery. Magistrates, clerks, even church officials who falsified parish records."

"How many families are implicated?" Freya asked, looking over my shoulder.

"At least a dozen prominent Devon families. Not enough to topple the government like Victoria claimed, but enough to cause significant social and financial upheaval in the region." I photographed each document with my phone. "And evidence that the cover-up continued into the modern era—people who knew the truth and actively suppressed it."

"Including people still alive today?"

"Including Gerald Winters, who handled the historical society's finances and made sure certain acquisitions never became public." I found another packet with more recent documents. "And Dr. Penrose, who apparently knew about the forgeries but chose academic discretion over revelation."

"Dr. Penrose?" Freya looked shocked. "But he helped us! He gave you information about Victoria!"

"After my great-aunt died and it became clear the truth was coming out anyway," I realized. "He positioned himself as helpful to avoid suspicion, but look at this—" I showed her a letter dated six months earlier. "He tried to convince my great-aunt to destroy the evidence entirely."

The scope of the conspiracy was larger and more complex than I'd imagined. Not just historical crimes, but ongoing cover-ups involving people I'd trusted.

"We need to get this to Drake immediately," I said, gathering the documents. "And we need to—"

The shop door chimed, and I looked up to see Dr. Penrose standing in the entrance, his expression grim.

"Miss Hampton," he said quietly, stepping inside and locking the door behind him. "I see you've found what Malcolm was protecting."

"Dr. Penrose." I tried to keep my voice calm while positioning myself between him and the documents. "We were just about to call DI Drake."

"I'm afraid that won't be possible." He produced a small pistol from his coat pocket. "Those documents represent the end of everything my family has built over generations. I simply cannot allow that."

"Your family?" Freya squeaked.

"The Penroses have held academic positions at prestigious institutions for over a century," he explained, his scholarly demeanor intact despite the weapon. "All based on recommendations and patronage from families whose legitimacy your great-aunt was determined to destroy. When their reputations fall, ours falls with them."

"So you helped Victoria kill her?" I asked, pieces falling into place.

"I provided the historical context that convinced her action was necessary. The foxglove was her idea—rather poetic, given your great-aunt's love of English gardens." He gestured with the pistol toward the documents. "Now please step away from those papers. There's been quite enough death already, but I will do what's necessary to protect my family's legacy."

Hardy chose that moment to emerge from behind a bookshelf, spotted Dr. Penrose, and began barking with unusual aggression. The distraction was enough for me to grab the heavy brass compass and swing it toward Penrose's gun hand.

The weapon discharged harmlessly into the ceiling as he stumbled backward, and Freya threw herself at the door, shouting for help at the top of her lungs. Within seconds, the patrol officers who'd been discretely watching the shop burst through the door.

Dr. Penrose sat on the floor holding his wrist, looking more like a defeated academic than a dangerous conspirator. The gun lay several feet away, and the precious documents were scattered but safe.

"Well," I said to Hardy, who was still barking triumphantly, "I guess you earned your keep today."

As the police secured the scene and called for Drake, I reflected on how wrong I'd been about almost everyone involved. The real conspiracy wasn't Victoria acting alone—it was a network of supposedly respectable people protecting centuries of lies.

But at least now, finally, the truth could be told.

23

Three hours later, DI Drake sat across from me in the bookshop's reading area, looking both exhausted and grimly satisfied as she reviewed the documents we'd recovered from the compass.

"Dr. Penrose has been quite cooperative since his arrest," she reported. "Apparently prison is less appealing than academic disgrace. He's provided names, dates, and details about the entire network."

"How extensive was it?" I asked, still processing the revelation that people I'd trusted had been actively working against us.

"Twelve families directly implicated in the original document forgeries, with another eight involved in the modern cover-up." Drake consulted her notes. "Not quite the regional apocalypse Victoria Ashford claimed, but significant enough to affect property values, political positions, and social standing throughout Devon."

"And Victoria herself?"

"Still missing, along with two accomplices we've now identified—a London lawyer specializing in property law and a document forger who's been creating false provenance for questionable antiques." Drake's expression hardened. "They have resources and expertise, which makes them more dangerous than I anticipated."

"But you have the evidence now," Freya pointed out. "Even if they eliminate us, the truth's already out."

"Which is exactly what makes you most vulnerable," Drake replied bluntly. "Desperate people take desperate actions. I'm keeping you under protection until we locate them."

"For how long?" I asked. "I can't hide indefinitely. The bookshop needs to reopen, Malcolm needs support during his recovery, and frankly, I refuse to let Victoria Ashford dictate how I live my life."

Drake studied me for a moment. "You've changed since I first met you. Less naive, more determined."

I wasn't naive, that was her assumption about my American upbringing. "More stubborn, you mean."

"More willing to fight for what matters." She smiled slightly. "Which is admirable but potentially suicidal given our current situation."

Before I could respond, Malcolm appeared in the doorway, supported by Elliot and looking pale but determined. His release from hospital had been expedited once the doctors realized he might be in continued danger and needed more protection than the hospital could provide.

"Miss Hampton," he greeted me with formal warmth. "I understand you solved my little puzzle."

"With Freya's help and Hardy's intervention," I replied, gesturing to the corgi who was lounging smugly near the compass. "Though I'm still amazed you managed to hide everything so cleverly."

"Your great-aunt taught me that the best hiding places

are in plain sight," he said, accepting the chair Elliot brought him. "She would be proud of your persistence in seeking the truth."

"Even if that truth is going to complicate a lot of lives?"

"Especially then." Malcolm's expression grew serious. "Comfortable lies serve no one except those who benefit from deception. Your great-aunt understood that historical justice sometimes requires contemporary discomfort."

Drake's phone buzzed with an urgent message. After reading it, her expression shifted to high alert.

"Victoria Ashford's car has been spotted heading back toward Tidehaven Cove," she announced. "I hoped that her message was simply a delaying tactic, but it seems she intends to be here at the end. All units are responding, but I want you somewhere more secure than the bookshop."

"Where?" Elliot asked. "My house is too isolated, the cottage is compromised, and anywhere else puts other people at risk."

"The church," Malcolm suggested unexpectedly. "St. Mary's has been a sanctuary for centuries. The building is solid stone, easily defensible, and Reverend Williams would never turn away people seeking protection."

"It's also where my great-aunt's memorial service was held," I added. "If Victoria wants a final confrontation, it's symbolically appropriate. And despite your reasonable objections, DI Drake, I think the only way to end this is with a face to face meeting."

Drake looked dubious. "I prefer secure locations I can control. And ones without civilians getting in the way."

"You can position officers around the building," Elliot pointed out. "And churches have multiple exits if evacuation becomes necessary. And I'm sure your constables will stop her on her way here."

"The tip came too late to do that. Now she's on by-roads, no cameras and lots of places to turn off." She gave us each a stern look. "Fine. But at the first sign of trouble, you follow my instructions without question."

Twenty minutes later, we were settled in St. Mary's nave while police took positions around the medieval building. Reverend Williams had welcomed us with the promised support. Settling us in, providing tea and expressing quiet confidence that "sanctuary would be honored."

"It's peaceful here," Freya observed, looking around at the stone arches and stained glass windows that had witnessed centuries of village life. "Hard to imagine violence in a place like this."

"Violence has visited many churches throughout our history," Malcolm replied soberly. "But so has justice, forgiveness, and redemption. Perhaps all three will find their place here tonight."

As evening approached, we maintained vigil in the ancient building. Drake coordinated with her officers via radio while the rest of us tried to appear casual despite the tension. The dogs settled near the altar, apparently sensing the sacred nature of the space and behaving with unusual dignity.

At precisely nine o'clock, my phone rang. Victoria's number.

"Hello, Ginny," she said, her voice eerily calm. "I see you've chosen your ground well. Very symbolic—seeking sanctuary after destroying so many lives."

"I haven't destroyed anything," I replied, putting the call on speaker so the others could hear. "I've just revealed truths that were already there."

"Truths that will ruin innocent people whose only crime was being born into families with complicated histories."

Victoria's voice carried genuine anguish. "Do you under-stand what you've unleashed? Children who will lose their homes, elderly people who will see their family names disgraced, communities that will be torn apart by ancient grievances?"

"Those are consequences of the original lies, not of revealing them," I replied firmly. "My great-aunt didn't create this situation—she just refused to perpetuate it."

"Your great-aunt was an idealistic fool who prioritized abstract justice over human compassion," Victoria snapped. "Just like you."

"If protecting historical truth makes me a fool, I'm comfortable with that label."

A long pause, then Victoria's voice grew colder. "Are you comfortable with being a dead fool? Because that's what you'll be if you don't destroy those documents and abandon this crusade."

"The documents are already with the authorities," Drake interjected, speaking toward my phone. "Threatening Miss Hampton won't change that."

"Detective Inspector Drake," Victoria acknowledged. "How many officers do you have surrounding the church? Enough to stop three determined people with nothing left to lose?"

Through the windows, I could see movement in the churchyard—shadows that weren't quite right, figures moving between the ancient headstones.

"Victoria," I said, trying to keep my voice steady, "it's over. The truth is out, the evidence is secured, and you can't change that by hurting more people."

"Can't I? History is written by survivors, Ginny." She laughed like she hadn't a care in the world. "If the people who know the truth don't survive to tell it, perhaps different truths will emerge."

"There are police everywhere. You can't—"

The line went dead as every light in the church suddenly went out.

Emergency lighting flickered on, casting eerie shadows through the nave as Drake barked orders into her radio. Outside, we could hear shouts and the sound of running feet.

"Stay low," Drake commanded, drawing her weapon. "They're trying to flush us out."

But instead of storming the building, Victoria's voice echoed from speakers that had been somehow connected to the church's sound system.

"Ginny Hampton," the amplified voice announced, "you have a choice. Walk out of that church alone, and your friends will be safe. We'll discuss this like civilized people, and perhaps we can reach an accommodation that serves everyone's interests."

"Don't even consider it," Elliot said immediately.

"It's obviously a trap," Freya added. "She can't do anything if we stay here."

But Malcolm was studying us. His mind running through the details. "Miss Hampton," he said quietly, "what would your great-aunt do?"

I knew the answer immediately. She would walk out there, because she believed that facing uncomfortable truths was always preferable to hiding from them. She would trust that justice, however imperfect, was worth personal risk.

"I'm going out there," I decided, not exactly comfortable with putting myself in danger, but exceedingly sure I would protect my friends.

"Absolutely not," Drake said firmly. "That's not an option."

"It's the only option that doesn't put everyone else at risk," I countered. "Victoria's right about one thing—this is between us now. She killed my great-aunt, and she needs to face the consequences of that choice."

"You're not a police officer," Drake reminded me. "You're a civilian under my protection."

"I'm someone who inherited more than just a bookshop," I replied, standing up despite the protests of everyone around me. "I inherited a responsibility to finish what my great-aunt started."

Before anyone could stop me, I walked toward the church door, my heart hammering but my resolve firm. Behind me, I could hear Drake coordinating with her officers, Elliot cursing creatively, and Freya calling my name.

I stepped out into the moonlit churchyard, where Victoria Ashford waited beside my great-aunt's memorial marker, flanked by two men I didn't recognize.

"Hello, Victoria," I said, surprised by how calm my voice sounded. "Ready to end this?"

"I've been ready since the moment your great-aunt decided to destroy everything I've worked to preserve," she replied. "The question is whether you're wise enough to prevent further tragedy."

"The only tragedy here is that three people died to protect lies, possibly more over the years since the original crime," I said firmly. "That ends now."

"Does it?" Victoria smiled coldly and raised what appeared to be a small explosive device. "Last chance, Ginny. Recant your story, discredit the documents, or watch this medieval church and everyone in it join your great-aunt in whatever comes after."

I looked at the device, at Victoria's desperate expression, at the armed men beside her. Then I looked at the memorial marker for my great-aunt, and I knew exactly what she would expect me to say. "No," I said simply. "The truth stands."

Victoria's finger moved toward the device's trigger—and froze as red laser dots appeared on all three conspirators simultaneously.

"Armed police!" Drake's voice boomed from multiple speakers. "Drop your weapons and get on the ground!"

The next few seconds passed in a blur of action. Victoria's accomplices immediately surrendered, but she clutched the explosive device with desperate determination.

"You don't understand!" she screamed. "The damage this will cause—"

"Will be the consequence of choices made long ago," I interrupted. "Choices that weren't your ancestors to make then and aren't yours to make now."

For a moment, Victoria stared at me with something that might have been respect. Then her shoulders slumped in defeat, and she carefully set the device on the ground. "I tried," she said quietly as the police moved in. "I tried to protect everyone."

"You tried to protect the wrong things," I replied. "And you destroyed good people in the process." As the words came out I heard my aunt's voice echoing in my head.

As Victoria was led away in handcuffs, I stood in the ancient churchyard surrounded by people who had become my chosen family—Drake, Malcolm, Freya, Elliot, and even Reverend Williams, who had emerged to check on his sanctuary.

"It's finished," Malcolm said, placing a gentle hand on

my shoulder. "You did a very brave thing. I am glad you inherited her estate."

"No," I corrected, looking at my great-aunt's memorial. "Now it begins. Now we tell the story properly."

The truth would indeed complicate lives and challenge assumptions. But it would also honor the memory of people who had died protecting historical justice, and it would ensure that future generations understood the real cost of both lies and truth.

My great-aunt's legacy was secure. The bookshop would continue. And Tidehaven Cove would finally face its past honestly, whatever the consequences. In the end, that was exactly what she would have wanted.

EPILOGUE

Two months later, I stood in the bookshop arranging a display of local history books, reflecting on how much had changed since that morning when I'd found Thornbury's body among the scattered manuscripts. The shop hummed with quiet contentment—customers browsing peacefully, Malcolm consulting with a visiting researcher, and Freya helping a family choose books for their holiday reading.

"Any regrets?" Elliot asked, appearing beside me with Austen and Hardy on leads. He'd taken on the afternoon walk and my delightful loyal corgis had adopted him as a member of their pack.

"About which part?" I replied, accepting enthusiastic corgi kisses. "Inheriting a bookshop, solving multiple murders, or agreeing to keep quiet about royal document fraud?"

"All of it, I suppose." He knelt to remove the leashes from the dog's collars. Austen jumped on an unoccupied chair, and Hardy wandered toward the back to sniff out Captain.

I considered the question seriously. The past two

months had been unlike anything I could have imagined when I'd first arrived in Tidehaven Cove seeking a quiet life among books.

The official story, as agreed upon during several very polite but firm meetings with representatives of Her Majesty's government, was that Dr. Reginald Thornbury had been killed during a burglary gone wrong. Victoria Ashford, distraught over the violence in her adopted community, had suffered a mental breakdown leading to increasingly erratic behavior resulting in a series of criminal acts. The historical documents in question had been deemed "interesting but inconclusive" by Crown historians and quietly transferred to appropriate archives.

"No regrets about the official version," I said finally. "The families involved have faced appropriate consequences—just privately rather than publicly."

And they had. The Ashford property developments had been quietly dissolved, with assets redirected to historical preservation charities. The Penrose family had lost their academic positions and social standing within relevant circles. Other implicated families had found their planning applications denied, their government contracts terminated, and their children mysteriously rejected from prestigious schools and universities.

Justice had been served—British style, with understatement and discretion rather than public trials and newspaper headlines.

"The memorial service was beautiful," Malcolm observed, joining our conversation. "Your great-aunt would have appreciated the turnout."

The official memorial—when her body was returned to her burial site—for Vivian Hampton-Davies had drawn representatives from universities, historical societies, and government departments, all praising her "dedicated schol-arship" and "invaluable contributions to local history." What they didn't mention was that her research had quietly prompted the most extensive review of historical land grants in centuries.

"She got what she wanted," I replied. "The truth came out, even if not the way she originally planned."

I nodded at DI Drake who walked through the front door dressed in what I assumed was her civilian clothes, jeans, teeshirt with a graphic flower design, and sandals. She scanned the other shoppers as she joined us.

"And you got what you needed," Freya added, as she rang in a large order of children's books for a harried mother. "A purpose, a community, and enough excitement to last several lifetimes. I'm so glad you weren't frightened away!"

"About that excitement," Drake said with her character-istic directness. Her transition to the county's historical crimes unit had suited her perfectly. "I have a proposition."

"Please tell me it doesn't involve more murders," I said with mock alarm—to be honest, not quite as mock as I wished.

"Nothing so dramatic. But it's come to my attention there's a regional book fair being organized for next autumn—'Devon Literary Heritage Festival.' They're looking for someone to coordinate the rare books and historical manuscripts section." Her slight smile suggested she knew exactly what my answer would be. "Someone with recent experience in historical document authen-tication."

I exchanged glances with Malcolm and Freya, both of whom were watching with barely concealed excitement.

"A book fair?" I repeated.

"Think of it as expanding your brand," Freya urged.

"'Hampton Books: Where History Comes Alive.' Though hopefully not literally this time."

"Terrible slogan," Malcolm observed dryly. "Though the opportunity has merit. Regional book fairs showcase the finest in literary heritage while connecting serious collectors with reputable dealers."

"Plus," Drake added casually, "it would position you as the go-to expert for historical document verification in the Southwest. Useful for preventing future... unpleasantness. It would make my job easier to have an expert."

The offer was tempting. Three months ago, I'd been a displaced corporate refugee. Now I was being invited to help shape the region's literary culture while serving as an unofficial guardian against historical fraud. My previous experience with Hartwell & Associates Publishing would be of enormous help in organizing an event.

"What about the shop?" I asked. "We can't neglect our primary business."

"The fair would be excellent publicity," Malcolm pointed out. "And Freya's online sales initiatives have made us less dependent on foot traffic. It would be an asset to have an annual book fair. You can make that a reality."

"Plus, autumn is perfect timing," Freya added. "I'll have finished my degree by then and could take on more responsibility here."

Before I could respond, the shop bell chimed, admitting Elspeth from the tea shop with her usual dramatic flair.

"Emergency!" she announced breathlessly. "Mrs. Weatherby's cat has been missing for three days, and she's convinced someone's stolen him for his supposed psychic abilities!"

We all stared at her for a moment.

"His what abilities?" I asked faintly. I thought I understood the quirks of my new home.

"Psychic abilities! Apparently, he predicted the last three village council election results by choosing between different food bowls." Elspeth lowered her voice conspiratorially. "She wants to hire you as a detective to find him."

"I'm not actually a detective," I protested. "I run a bookshop."

"Tell that to the woman whose historical documents you authenticated, whose murder you solved, and whose criminal conspiracy you exposed," Drake observed with amusement. "Face it, Ginny—you've acquired a reputation."

"For solving mysteries involving books and historical documents," I clarified. "Not missing cats."

"Missing psychic cats," Freya corrected with obvious glee. "This is definitely going in our promotional materials."

"We are not adding pet detective services to our business model," I said firmly. "Especially if we are taking on this book fair project."

"Why not?" Malcolm asked mildly. "You are always telling me to be more flexible. The village clearly has confidence in your investigative abilities. And think of the social media possibilities. Not that I will take part of course."

I looked around at their expectant faces—Drake with her professional interest, Malcolm with his scholarly curiosity, Freya with her irrepressible enthusiasm, Elliot with his veterinary expertise, and even Elspeth with her gossip network connections. If I was going to create a detective agency, it would include all of these people. And despite the claim of extrasensory abilities, losing a pet like that would be heartbreaking.

"Fine," I sighed. "I'll look into Mrs. Weatherby's missing

psychic cat. But only because it's probably hiding in someone's shed, not because I'm actually a detective."

As the afternoon progressed and we dealt with the usual
combination of customers, community members, and
requests for obscure books that had become our daily
routine, I reflected on how perfectly this captured my new
life. Historical research balanced with immediate problems,
serious scholarship mixed with village eccentricity, and the
constant challenge of maintaining a bookshop while
somehow becoming the person people called when unusual
situations required attention.

My great-aunt had left me more than just a business and
a mystery to solve. She'd left me a role in the community, a
responsibility to protect both truth and the people affected
by it, and the understanding that sometimes the most
important justice happens quietly, behind the scenes, where
it can do the most good with the least harm.

The Crown's intervention hadn't diminished the victory
—it had simply ensured that justice was served with appropriate discretion. The guilty had faced consequences, the
innocent had been protected, and the community had been
preserved.

Elliot was waiting for me to join him for dinner at the
end of the day. He held the dog's leashes while we tidied up.
"So, book fair coordinator, historical document expert, and
now pet detective. What's next?"

"Hopefully, a quiet evening with good food, good
company, and absolutely no mysteries requiring investigation," I replied.

"Where's the fun in that?" Freya grinned.

As I looked around the bookshop—at the shelves filled
with stories, the reading nooks where community gathered,
the comfortable chaos of a well-loved space—I realized she

was right. My great-aunt had given me more than just an inheritance. She'd given me a purpose that perfectly combined my love of books, my developing appreciation for community, and my apparently natural talent for uncovering inconvenient truths.

A book fair is a big job to organize, but Ginny is up for it. Big egos, professional infighting, that's all part of the deal. A dead body not so much. The next book in the Pages and Paws series is Bound by Secrets.

If you enjoyed reading Death on the Bookshelf please consider helping other readers to find the story by leaving a review.

POPPY BRIDGEMAN

FREE BOOK

Claim your copy of The Charleston Diary when you sign up for my newsletter. Learn how Ginny solved a case of forgery before she headed to the peace and tranquility of Tidehaven Cove.

ALSO BY POPPY

For more books by Poppy Bridgeman
scan the QR code below.

ABOUT POPPY BRIDGEMAN

Hi, I'm Poppy Bridgeman, the cozy mystery alter ego of Canadian author P A Wilson. Poppy was "born" because sometimes stories need a gentler touch—with a little magic, a dash of humor, and plenty of sleuthing spirit.

As Poppy, I write the *Witch of Henbane Island* series (where witches and festivals collide with mysteries), the *EB Eats Culinary Mysteries* (a small-town diner, a determined heroine, and murder on the menu), and the *Pages & Paws Bookstore Mysteries* (a Devon bookshop, two mischievous corgis, and plenty of secrets tucked between the shelves).

When I'm not tangled in my characters' escapades, I'm happily tangled in yarn—I knit, weave, and doodle in sketchbooks between writing sessions. I also love to travel, finding inspiration for charming settings, quirky characters, and suspicious strangers wherever I go.

Home base is the Vancouver area, where I juggle writing as both Poppy and P A Wilson. Whichever name is on the cover, I'm always chasing the next story.

ACKNOWLEDGMENTS

People think that the process of writing is solitary. That's not the case for me. I have help from so many people it would be hard to acknowledge everyone, but I'll give it a try.

The support and inspiration I get from my writer's groups is incalculable. The Vancouver Writers Social Group opens my mind to other ways of telling a story. The Royal City Literary Arts Society gives me the opportunity to meet and share with other writers who have more knowledge than I do. The Other 11 Months group is where I learn about getting the words on the page. And my critique group who helps me find the best parts of the story I want to tell. Thanks to all of the members of these great groups.

Last of all, but definitely a huge part of the process, my beta readers. These are the people who love stories and are willing, and more than able, to tell me if my finished story is ready for you, my readers.